Religion

and

Democracy

South Sudan, Faith, Hope and Love

By Garang Malong

This book is here to create and strengthen Christians and Muslims of South Sudan and unite all Faiths. The suffering of the people of South Sudan either Muslims or Christians, Hindus or animist was political based, but the new generation should forgive one another and ensure the history doesn't repeat itself…

This book is to highlight the challenges our generation and the generations of our fathers underwent and that our children should live in peace as one people of one nation and not categorize them based on religious grounds or race.

For the memories of our fallen heroes and heroines in all conflicts in the last six decades… we can only show love to them if we love their families, our families, our country and all inhabitants of South Sudan.

"A nation without God's guidance is a nation without order. Happy are those who keep God's law!"

- Proverbs 29:18

May whoever reads this book receive blessings and discover their inner faith.

- Garang Malong Awan Anei

Table of Contents

Topic Three

Part Two

Topic Four

Part Three

Topic Five

Preface

THIS BOOK WAS WRITTEN from my concern over the huge differences in South Sudan between traditional believers and Christians. Yet more important, it is about teaching our people the word of God—people who have continually been victims of Sharia law in Sudan.

Sudan is an Islamic country and a member of the Arab League. Before receiving our Independence on 9th July 2011, the people in South Sudan had no voice. Against their will, they were at war with other Christian states. As a member of the Arab League, the government in Khartoum led them to war. Today, as the Republic of South Sudan, we want to stand categorically as a Christian state and preach the word of our LORD Jesus Christ to the people of South Sudan who have for so long been denied their rights as Christians.

The Christianity practiced today is what the missionaries taught them years ago. Since that time, there have been no missionaries to help strengthen the faith of the people.

This book chronicles the background of South Sudan and her struggle of being Christian believers in an Islamic environment. Emphasis is placed upon learning from our history—that politics and religion should not mix, and that politics has failed to protect the Christian people of South Sudan. The political class should lead all people equally without interfering with their religious beliefs and norms. South Sudan seceded from Sudan because it failed to separate the two institutions.

I envision a solution where all people have religious freedom, and not all people are politicians. The independent state of South Sudan should be a secular state with separation of religion and politics.

This book seeks to unite the Christians and bring the Word of Jesus Christ back to the lost population of traditional believers. Our people have been marginalized and have not had an opportunity to go to school; hence, have not been exposed to the world. My desire is to bring them up to date with the Christian unity that will defend the rights of the majority. Muslims are competing for our people in an effort to turn them to the Islam religion, but Christianity will help unify those in the villages and we can then learn from one another. A Christian coalition is a way in which our Christian population can have a voice in the conversation of democracy through one channel on the national agenda and Christian manifesto.

The Christians of South Sudan need to be guided and led by true believers to unify them in one faith to serve Christ. This book can serve as a guideline to encourage South Sudanese Christians to write and document their religious life, as well as help strengthen the faith of Christians worldwide. In this book I have shared my vision, thoughts, and dreams for the South Sudan we desire. I firmly believe that it is possible through love, faith and hope.

In addition, I have related some visions I received from the Lord in dreams that were confirmed in Biblical Scripture. Through Christ, we get to see the glory of God—His love and the forgiveness of our sins.

- Garang Malong
Nairobi, Kenya
14th March, 2020

Part One

Topic One

Introduction to South Sudan

SOUTH SUDAN IS A multi-denominational country located in proximity of East Africa and North Africa. After receiving independence from Sudan on July 9, 2011, it has joined the East Africa community. South Sudan is a country of multi-denominational country. The national language is English and the widely spoken language is Arabic. Other recognized national languages are Dinka, Nuer, Shilluk, Zande, Bari, Murle and Luo. The country has sixty-four ethnic groups and more than sixty different languages.

South Sudan is bordered by Kenya to the southeast, Ethiopia to the east, Uganda to the south, the Democratic Republic of the Congo to the southwest, the Central Africa Republic to the west and Sudan to the north. South Sudan has the largest swamp region in Africa, called Sudd, formed by the White Nile. The country has the largest wild animal migration in the world. Boma National Park is described as three times larger than Maasai Mara National Park, and then we have Southern National Park and Bandingilo National Park. The landscape of South Sudan is primarily grassland, swamps and tropical forests. The Imatong Mountains include Mount Kinyeti, the highest mountain in South Sudan at 10,456 ft. (3,187 m).

The country has abundant resources, with petroleum being the major source of government revenues at 98%. River Nile is the main natural feature. South Sudan is blessed with natural resources such as gold, uranium, zinc, copper, chromium, tungsten, mica, silver and hydropower.

As a South Sudanese, we obtained our independence from Sudan, an Islamic state, primarily because of our different faiths, which caused war between the two regions. The power struggle over which religion would control the country's resources was another factor in our fifty years of civil war.

South Sudan was a British colony, though they exchanged hand with French colony, the missionaries introduced Catholicism as the major denomination in the country. But even after the Catholic introduction, and having many who were born Catholic, the majority are still animist. They follow their traditional beliefs and norms.

South Sudan has gone through much suffering and torture—from her own people, her own government, and at the hands of colonizers who actually did not have much interest in southern Sudan but only in Sudan. They colonized North Sudan and administered the south from the north. Sudan first declared as an Islamic state, not considering the Christian population in the country. Then the president introduced Sharia law, which conflicted with the Christianity of the majority of those in the south of Sudan.

The government that was formed after the colonizers left never paid much attention to the lives in the south, and Maram took over the leadership. The Southerners did not have many people who attended colonial schools, and the few who were assimilated into the Maram-led government with even little voice for their people. Other than being denied the freedom to worship, they were deprived of the economic benefits of the country. South Sudan suffered in the hands of the North Sudan government for five decades. Although the people of South Sudan held on to Christianity and their traditional beliefs, their mother country was marginalizing their own citizens and Christian nations did not come fast enough to rescue them.

There were no priests to teach the word of God and the majority of the people were not educated to read the bible and interpret it to the population. There was a total breakdown of learning institutions in southern Sudan. There were no schools, because the mission schools closed when the war broke out. The government in Khartoum made sure that all the teachers and other services were locked down in southern Sudan because, they claimed, they demanded their rights. The only recourse for those who wanted/ needed an education was first to become a Muslim. Just as Sudan was governed by Egypt before gaining independence in 1956, Sudan did the same to the people of South Sudan and controlled them from Khartoum.

The burning of churches and the five-decade civil war drove the Christians south, causing them to leave their ancestral home and become displaced persons. This ultimately resulted in referendum and an independent state of South Sudan. The Christian south came together and fought to gain independence from the North Sudan government at the cost of more than two million lives and thousands displaced. South Sudan has paid dearly for her Independence.

Unbelievably, after gaining independence from Sudan, many of the people of South Sudan became refugees, and many more are in exile due to poor leadership from their own leaders—the ones we ourselves elected in 2010. The conflict in the South is not about religion this time; rather it is a struggle of greed, tribalism and the control of political power and resources. The leadership divided the country into tribes and then confiscated the communities, either over land dispute or control of resources and power.

Any person appointed by the president is given state powers to suppress a neighboring community. While the president watches, the government officials use the state institutions and law enforcement to kill and loot. Cattle raiders are given the latest guns of the national security to raid other communities. This has sent thousands of marginalized families and communities into refugee camps in the neighboring countries. While the youth are used as the agents of these conflicts, the politicians loot the national budget and with their newly-found wealth, send their families oversees.

The South Sudanese—men, women and children—are facing genocide at the hands of their own government. The people can emerge strong if there is a change of leadership and the new leadership unites the people, hence creating a future of reconciliation and a rebuilding of the country.

At this time, there are not more than ten Christian churches in South Sudan, but these few churches have strong faith in the Christianity they fought five decades to defend.

Unfortunately, some "churches" have preyed on the uneducated population and have robbed our people of their money through "teachers" who have neither the wisdom nor the knowledge to teach the word of God. If one day we build a church, it will unify the Christian population of South Sudan with one faith and hope, to serve one Christ Jesus. As the Bible tells us, the people of Cush will only be forgiven by God if they all go to Mt. Zion and repent of their sins. All faiths, we should live as one people one nation and serve one Living God and repent as one people but with different faiths house.

The living God has persevered in South Sudan with a purpose, and I believe that purpose is in the independence we gained in the twenty-first century. God protected this region, its heritage, and the vast land that no human foot has stepped upon since creation of the universe.

In-depth accounting of the struggle and suffering of the South Sudanese to gain independence can be found in several other books, including my book, *Why South Sudan Matters.*

The Beginning of Christianity and Persecution

Christianity has had a long history in the region of Sudan known today as South Sudan. In the 2nd century when Christian missionaries came to Sudan, they brought Coptic Christianity and dwelt in the ancient Nubia Kingdom and Cush Kingdom that are now the Dinka and Nuer people. South Sudan was dominated by the traditional belief (animist), and that made it hard for the missionaries to settle there. Moreover, the central authority of South Sudan was chiefdom and that made it hard to spread Christianity in that ethnic division.

Early in the middle ages, the Byzantine Emperor Justinian 1, who reigned from 527 to 565, had a lot of interest in the Cush Kingdom and Nubia Kingdom. He made that region a Christian stronghold so that he could access South Sudan and spread Christianity. Northern Sudan was primarily known to be a Christian region by 580 AD, making Christianity the official religion of Sudan before the coming of the Islamic religion.

Coptic Christianity was widely spread in Sudan and was the dominant religion of the Nubia and Nilotic (Dinka and Nuer) of Sudan until the 7th century when it fell to the Islamic invasions. Christianity was under threat with the spread of the new religion and expansion of the Arabs in the region. South Sudan remained untouched and maintained the traditional religion and beliefs of the Nilotic people.

During the 19th century when the British missionaries came, they reintroduced Christianity to the people of southern Sudan. However, because multi-ethnic southern Sudan rejected the spread of Christianity, the colonials and the missionaries had very little interest in South Sudan, and the British Imperial authority expended few resources and limited missionary activities in the region. The first Catholic mission was established in southern Sudan in 1852. The Church of England and the Anglican Communion also taught Christianity to the people of southern Sudan.

Later, the Sudan Interior Church was introduced in the country in 1937. Subsequently, southern Sudan became a hub of Christianity in the region and the Africa Inland Church was opened in 1949. The spread of Christianity and the spread of Islam caused the two factions to compete for the traditional believers of southern Sudan—they were not to be left to their indigenous beliefs, but to turn either Islamic or Christian. The struggle and the friction between the three religious groups . . . traditional believers (Animists), Christians or the Muslims that controlled Sudan after gaining their independence in 1956, caused the civil war.

The independence of Sudan in 1956 marked the beginning of southern Sudan's struggle and the persecution of the South Sudanese Christians.

The regime in Khartoum failed to convert the southern Sudanese to Islam, so waged war on them. The government ordered all foreign missionaries to leave South Sudan in 1964. The government wanted to wipe out the South Sudanese, so they asked the missionaries to leave their missions and move to north Sudan until the war was over. This had an ill effect on the South Sudanese who were just beginning to learn about Christianity, and having the Bible translated into the language they could understand. Although the civil war with north Sudan united the multi-ethnic South Sudan, there was tremendous persecution of the Christians and damage to their villages.

When the people of South Sudan rebelled against the regime in Khartoum, the Catholic Church and Anglican Church in Khartoum had already seen what was happening in various parts of South Sudan—the killing of the Christians and persecution of pastors and church leaders. As a result, their leaders in Khartoum declared not to leave Sudan and condemned the persecution of Christians in South Sudan. They said that they would not abandon them, as God had revealed to them that Christians of South Sudan were under threat of sharia law.

In the more than 50 years of the civil war, many villages were burned and properties were looted. Pastors were persecuted with church leaders and churches were burned down. Hospitals and Christian schools were destroyed. All of the missionaries' bases were bombed and Christian worshippers at Sunday services were threatened. The estates that were dwelling places for the Christians were destroyed, and the Christians killed. Those who escaped the persecution joined the rebellion in the bush, led by the South Sudanese.

Raids on Southern Sudan villages by the Maram militia resulted in the abduction of approximately 200,000 women and children, who were then enslaved in northern Sudan. A few have reunited with their families, many have died in slavery, and others have not yet been found—even after the Independence of South Sudan. A

Maram girl was sentenced to death for marrying a South Sudanese Christian. In May of 2014, *after* our Independence of 2011, a woman was sentenced to a hundred lashes for "adultery" by marrying a Nilotic Christian of South Sudan, and later imprisoned. Respect for all people and their choice of religion is paramount for the development and peace of South Sudan.

In 1980, there were only 1.6 million Christians in Southern Sudan. Since seceding from north Sudan, the number of Christians has increased to over 11 million. However, the Christian denominations are not based in South Sudan. They operate from Uganda or Kenya. Their clergy are unpaid. The Christians have no money for offerings, as there is no support from the government of South Sudan. According to the U.S. State Department's International Religious Freedom Report of 2012, the majority of South Sudan's population adheres to Christianity.

Modern Christianity is appreciated by the people of South Sudan. The majority are Roman Catholic (nearly two million Roman Catholics with seven dioceses across the Republic of South Sudan) or Anglican Church, and some in the Episcopal Church of Sudan. The population in general identify as Christian, even if they do not attend a Christian church service. They may be animist, but the war that was fought between Maram and Christians before gaining our independence categorically united South Sudanese as Christian—even those who are not.

Many Christians in the world have come to South Sudan in support of the marginalized South Sudanese against the Maram oppression from north Sudan. This has resulted in the spread of the gospel of Jesus Christ and the introduction of more churches. Some, but not all, of the churches other than the Roman Catholic and Anglican Churches are as follows:

1. Coptic Orthodox Church of Alexandria
2. Africa Inland Church
3. Ethiopia Orthodox Tewahedo Church
4. Eritrean Orthodox Tewahedo Church
5. Apostolic Church
6. Greek Orthodox Church
7. New Apostolic
8. Jehovah Witnesses
9. International Church of the Nazarene
10. Seventh Day Adventist Church
11. Presbyterian Church of the Sudan
12. Sudan Presbyterian Evangelical Church
13. Sudan Pentecostal Church
14. Sudan Church of Christ
15. Sudan Interior Church

A large number of the people of South Sudan are abandoning their traditional religion (animist) for Christianity and Islamic. Those who have not are the aged in villages where Christianity has not spread, and those in towns who may have heard of Christianity, but have little faith because of the high level of illiteracy in the country. Interpreters are needed for the people to be able to understand the Bible in their native language.

In order to allow the smooth running of government activities in the Republic of South Sudan, religion and politics should be separated. The struggle for our independence has united us as a nation—no longer as tribes or no religious group. We wish to learn from our experience with civil war and religious persecution. As followers of Jesus Christ, love for our neighbor should be in our hearts, putting religious differences aside. This will bring the peace we desire.

Religion and Democracy

Because South Sudan has suffered greatly under the heavy hand of religion. Government and religion must be separate entities and operated independently. South Sudan must have freedom of religion, where each person can and should worship God as he or she chooses.

As an independent, multi-denominational country, it is important that we guide our people in such a way that they are able to make their own faith choices, never mixing the state and religion. The religious leaders should lead the faith community and the politicians lead the political class. The people of South Sudan who come from a traditional (animist) background will need a great deal of guidance from the religious leaders. However, the state will need to set a national manifesto in collaboration with religious leaders in order that this innocent population not be misled because of their illiteracy.

South Sudan should be open to all religious communities, but guided by a national agenda and the national interest of the people of South Sudan. The crusades and Sabbath days should be respected and the country should be a secular state rooted in the Christian foundation. The Christians should respect and allow other religions to coexist and worship their God at will in a free and peaceful society.

Freedom of religion should allow an individual or a community, citizen or foreigner, to have his or her right to worship. As a people who have been denied our rights for many years, we need not deny others their rights of freedom to worship in a decent manner that does not interrupt the liberty of others. Although it is a fundamental human right, it is essential that the liberty of others and the public be considered.

A Message to My People

My people of South Sudan, as we thank God for His kind heart and mercy—we know that LORD, God Almighty has shown us his love and power. The victory of our promised land came from the Lord. He paid the price for us. He saved us, delivered us from our enemies and gave us a land to rule as free people, Cush People. We were slaves for fifty years in our land, and two million of our relatives and friends have been killed in this wasteful war. Thousands have been displaced from their ancestral homes and are in exile, others were lost in the vast forests of South Sudan. Many have been food to the wild animals and vultures.

The wasteful war has cost us lives and at last, God has remembered us and saved us as his own children. When peace came, the first light we saw was the introduction of multi-denomination to our communities and schools. That light shined so brightly, and we welcomed it like the prodigal son of the bible. Our people flocked into church, eagerly willing to learn the word of God.

Many of us were baptized and took Christian names. Others could take two names to be a true believer and we all eagerly accepted the God, our Lord Jesus. We learned that he died on the cross because of our sins, and that there were two kind of sins, sins of our ancestors which we are born with it and there are our sins that we commit daily. We were taught that baptism was a way in which our sins are washed away. We accepted it eagerly and we repented of our sins and accepted Jesus as LORD and as the Son of God and the Messiah.

For the prior fifty years, we worshipped our household gods and idols. No one came to our world to give us the word of God. Even the missionaries were afraid, as our people were not willing to change their ways—they consulted and received answers from their gods. But that was to keep them until the Messiah came as the savior of the world to deliver all people. The time has come for all of us to repent and turn to LORD, God Almighty, and that deliverance will save our country and our generations. **"A nation without God's guidance is a nation without order. Happy are those who keep God's law!**

Proverbs 29:18

The people who inflicted war on us did not have any reason to kill us, other than to force their ideologies and religion upon us. But now we have what we have been waiting for—free will. Christ Jesus has come to save us and the world with His blood that was poured on the cross. As we repent and become true Christians, we should not forget where we came from. The bible says, forgive and do not forget, as it might hurt you in the days to come.

Keeping our Christian history is very important. It gives us a good start in initiating our policies from a Christian perspective.

We South Sudanese voted for separation from the north—from the Maram ideologies. Some of us were 70 years old and had never voted—others of us were 30 and seeing a ballot box for the first time.

Our people voted for Independence, and with that came an introduction to democracy. That democracy should be the foundation of our leadership. God who saved us and gave us the land that He promised should be the founding father and the source of our knowledge and wisdom in uniting our country. God has shown us His love and power. It is time to leave our household gods and idols and turn to the true God.

We spent over fifty years fighting for freedom of religion. That freedom should not be restricted now. However, it is important to guide our people so they will be protected from greedy preachers and people seeking wealth. Freedom of religion can be misused and mislead the citizens. We do not want to lose this freedom because our enemies do not want us to celebrate our victory. Therefore, our "politics" should always give our Christians the right to assemble in an organized manner, and worshipping God should not be stopped under any circumstances.

The Spiritual Realm

The spiritual realm is the world beyond the normal world we see, or the realm inhabited by spirit, both good and evil of varies spiritual manifestation. The spiritual realm is the world of the prophets and magicians. Only those with God's powers can see what is happening in the realm. Most of the Spiritual writers concurred with the spiritual world was of tangible substance and a place consisting of "zones" or 'spheres."

A common Spiritual conception is that the Spirit world is inherently good and mostly related to truth-seeking and only few that are chosen or in Africa traditional, only inherited from family lineage. Africa believers and from the viewpoint of South Sudanese, Spiritual world is "A Home to the Soul." In the natural world, a person that experience the spirit world is a blissful, and considered a spiritual person who can tell others what is happening in the spirit and that can be useful in real life.

There is teleportation, the people who teleport are those who can visit the future and come back and tell of the future events. They have the capability to trace the past life and narrate it.

In the Spiritual realm, God exist and all the angels of God are always in the Spiritual world guiding the events and God will. God has created the universe and put human being in the face of the world to guide and protect its nature. He has given all rights to the mankind to make their decisions both right and wrong choices at will. When God created the mankind, he gave them a 'helper' as said by the Holy Spirit. The 'helper' and Holy Spirit were sent by God to guide his chosen people and defend them in all danger and troubles. There are several events in the Bible where Holy Spirit of God rescued and performed miracles to show the power of God. The Guardian Angels are seen in both our spiritual realm and on the natural world. They know what is going to happen in the future and they guide the mankind through the instincts to make right decisions.

As we try to discover the world that God created, we tend to find ourselves doing dangerous discoveries that have made many meet their death. With the guidance of our Holy Spirit, guiding our instincts we have made rational decisions escaping the death and age in peace. The old age is for the few historians. God has guided the new generation. The exploration of the world to understand God's creation has given us knowledge and it has also killed many scholars and researchers.

Each human being is assigned with two Guardian Angels from birth till their last breath. That means God has more Angels than our actually population. The Holy Spirit are given mankind and he is to guide us to fulfill our mission and what is required of us on this earth. As there is Chief Angel in the Spiritual world so is there a born leader in our society. The Chief Angel is powerful and sees the Living God and reports to our God, just like the angels of a young child see God daily. The good and bad spirits meet, interact and consult. When a right person is tested, God is always consulted through the spirit, just like the thieves, robbers, prostitutes, and magicians interact with good Christians, virgins, good hearted, spiritual leaders, good Samaritans and priests. We never know robbers until they are caught, though we interacted with them. The difference with the spiritual world is that the spirits know each other's territory and they can know when God is present. When Jesus met, a man infested with evil spirit, the evil spirit spoke out and said, "what do you want from me son of God, time is not yet for the Living God to take charge." That statement is from my memory from the years I watched the movie of Jesus.

That statement proves that the spirits know the presence of God and they all fear the power of God and so do they fear Angels of God and God's chosen people. Most of those who are chosen face a lot of obstacles to get to their destiny and that's always the evil spirit in the spiritual world that tends to delay and test their faith.

I have had vision where I met Jesus Christ and I met with the Angels of God. The land I met them was the spiritual world. It was not in any place that I know. God took me to the spiritual realm and gave me a message to bring back to the natural world. Due to what God had revealed to me and the knowledge that God had made me acquire through my Guardian Angels, I will make my readers understand the Spiritual realm.

As some of us are given Chief Angels, some are given Angels of knowledge, Angels of writing, Angels of wisdom to sing, Angels of business and farming while others given Angels of other expertise and gifts. The Bible said all humans are given different Holy Spirit that give them different talents. We are one in Holy Spirit as we are one in God but the Holy Spirit gives different gifts that we call talents.

There are three different worlds, the natural world, the Spirit world and the Heaven. The closest one is the natural world and few understand how the spiritual world work and we have no under-standing of Heaven even though there are a few who have been taken to heaven, the likes of Elijah was taken to heaven alive by a chariot of horses. The spiritual realm control the natural world and the spiritual realm is control from Heaven. They are a series of world that harvest its souls from the next world.

In our natural world, we plan for our visions and missions in order to realize our purpose on the universe. Our Guidance Angels who carry our files of our missions and visions on the universe guide our daily duties that we fulfill them without the evil spirit taking charge and mislead us. That brings a competition over souls between the evil and Angels of God. I believe that Angels meeting is always done to make the rest of the Guidance Angels make each and every person follow one person as a leader even when we do not agree as human, we can trust and believe on one person and that is one unifying leader or a symbol of unity.

When I was fired as a State government minister of Youth, Culture and Sports. I believe my Guardian Angels travelled to United States of America and spoke to the Guardian Angels of the person who later emailed me and saved my life.

As the tension and the threats of the governor who wanted me arrested and killed were eased off, I thought all was over, I was now safe. One of the security personnel later confessed, "we were told to pick you up at night, dress you up in military uniform, take you to the forest and kill you and later say, you rebelled against the government and that I was shooting at the government troops."

My life was in danger and I could not tell much when a telephone call was made to the governor telling him to stop harassing me and the plan to have me arrested and sent to Juba where allegation charges would be written against me and I would be executed for crimes I never committed. My Guardian Angels made roundtrips around the universe to find a solution that would save my life as my mission on earth had not yet began. Saving my life was of great importance to my Angels than my job, food and shelter.

When I received money, I booked for a transit in Juba to Nairobi from Northern Bahr el Ghazal, Awiel. The plane that was to pick us in Awiel delayed and I was worried that I would miss my flight.

It came two hours late to Awiel. All these times I was praying and calling on my God, to save me and not to lose the ticket, I could not have afforded another one. I spent another one and half hours airborne. I spent those hours sweating and praying in the plane. I knew I wouldn't make it to Nairobi as the security was arresting, killing Malong's supporters and looting his property. I was not sure what would be of me, his own son.

Everyone had checked in and boarded the plane. I was praying on a plane that was not moving any distance. I closed my eyes and kept praying knowing Kenya Airways never waits for anyone, but I was sure that with prayers it will wait for me and my family.

When the plane landed, I walked to Kenya Airways and boarded the plane and I found everyone seated waiting for me. I never heard any complain from any passenger for my delay. I came to Nairobi and I felt safe and relieved from all the danger and stress of gossip, safe from the greedy, thirsty security personnel who bred on innocent blood. I felt like I was in heaven.

I witnessed the spiritual realm and the natural world. When we can't explain the actions and events that take place then it's the spiritual realm that took control of the events of the natural world. I came without a house, not knowing where I am going. God was controlling my destiny; my Angels were tasked to provide all that was needed at my disposal at the right time of need.

The first few weeks I was hosted by a university classmate, who at one point, I hosted in South Sudan while I offered him a job of teaching in my high and primary school premises. He hosted me as I found my way on how I would survive in exile. Unplanned exile, just woke up and found myself on witch-hunt. Just like 'Job' in the Bible was tempted and the evil was told never to take away his life, I was in the same position.

I was alone in the foreign land; I was left with my angels and my God who has always stood with me and my safety. I lived like a God's Angel who only waited for instructions, my moves have always been defined by God for the time I have been in exile.

I did my second book, "**South Sudan: The Suffocation of a New Democracy**" while in exile trying to find solutions to the political unrest in my country. My first book being, "**Why South Sudan Matters.**" All that I wrote was not being read, our highly illiterate population were not exposed to books. Moreover, hatred had reached the bream, no one would read a book written by a rebel as that is how they labeled me and the youths who are opinionated about the bad governance and corruption in the country.

I left the country, South Sudan not as a rebel but as someone who sought safety in a foreign land. While in exile, I found a reason to accept the name rebel even when I was only an opinion writer. All opinion writers in South Sudan are never called opposition or academician rather they are labelled as rebels. Many have died because of such barbaric labelling. And if you don't accept you will still be killed by an unknown opposition, accepting the name makes it easy to know your category and group that you will count yourself in for your safety.

I have spent five years in exile and still counting, I can't tell how long it will take, I trust God is in control. The business that I initiated was left for dishonest people who could not get me any of my shares and if I sent someone they set them up with security and could be arrested for associating with rebels. A few have been arrested and I could not risk their lives anymore for my sake. I was left in exile for death and vultures of the streets to feast on me. God has never left me and my Angels have been kind and supportive. When I needed help my Angels brought forth what my heart desired though it has never been in abundant, but all that has always kept me safe and focused on my mission and vision. Fuel for my car, shelter and food on my table, and school fees adding headache to demanding rent.

In my second year of exile, God sent me visions and dreams of the future of South Sudan. I started to walk in the spiritual realm and all that I said was being revealed. I have written several visions/dreams that God has shown me and they have come to pass and more are still ahead. The truth of my Angels and what God showed me has been proven right by genocide that I was shown and it happen. God showed me the promised land that the people of South Sudan have not yet reached. God through his Angels gave me peace and who will lead the people of South Sudan and he will not come through war or elections rather through the will of the president to hand over power.

I moved from the city to the rural area where I thought I could afford and I still could not afford it. Life was proving unbearable in exile. I would advise others to never accept bad governance and corruption, I understand what all that has cost to the people of South Sudan especially women and innocent children. As I write this second book in exile, peace is still a song of war in my beloved country. The same people who called for peace are the same fueling the war, arming the illiterate youth to fight their course and mobilizing their ethnic groups to never accept a piece of the government cake. I am stuck and stranded in the middle of nowhere praying to God that brought me to exile to find me a solution and find a solution to my country.

I am still out here because God has a purpose for my life. There is a struggle in the spiritual realm between my Angels and evil who want to change the course of my destiny but God has not accepted. The good God still holds my destiny and purpose in his book in heaven. Many Christians should know that our Angels are God given and they have a purpose, none of us has evil guidance unless the one who comes from the world of evil.

The spiritual realm exists and as we struggle, our Angels are also fighting the evil that is stopping our blessings. God has blessings for each individual God has created. God is a good God; he plans good things to us and he has assigned his Angels to lead us right. Any problem that comes to us is not from God, God has always confirmed to us that he is a God of righteousness and our righteous God will never mix Himself with evil. No one has ever mixed good food with spoilt food and eaten, neither has anyone ever put human waste in his or her kitchen. If we can't put human waste in the kitchen, then there is no way our good God can put his creation in a test or any problem. The spiritual realm is real and God exist there so is evil. God protects all who love Him and follow his son Jesus Christ.

Topic Two:

Visions/Dreams and Biblical Comparisons

Good News Bible
Mathew 7:7-12
Ask, seek, knock

"Ask, and you will receive; seek, and you will find; knock, and the door will be opened to you. For everyone who asks will receive, and anyone who seeks will find, and the door will be opened to those who knock. Would any of you who are fathers give your son a stone when he asks for bread? Or would you give him a snake when he asks for a fish? Bad as you are, you know how to give good things to your children. How much more, then, will your Father in heaven give good things to those who ask him!

"Do for others what you want them to do for you: this is the meaning of the Law of Moses and of the teaching of the prophets."

Jesus Called Me My Friend,
And He Took Me to Heaven.
July, 2019
God vision on South Sudan

I pray every evening before I sleep, and as usual I kneel down to pray, praise the Lord and worship GOD. I give thanks and praises to my father in heaven. I pray for peace to prevail in South Sudan, as the country is in chaos, with millions displaced and thousands killed in tribal conflicts. I don't forget to pray for the people of South Sudan, and the beloved people of God, Israeli, Kenya my host country and the superpower, the United States of America, Europe and Middle East. I stay in exile, where I have no relative to lean on, no shoulder to cry on. I had to man up and turn to Lord Jesus when all seemed lost. All these happened after my father was released from house arrest and sent to exile. Then, his family was the next target to be killed or chased out of the country.

I have been in exile for five years and counting, without a job or any source of income. God has been faithful and kind to me. I had never lacked till this one time, I went for six months without paying rent, excused it to the pandemic but there was no income, all had come to a standstill. Thanks to God that he has always provided for my family. I couldn't tell what was happening, but there was no hope, no light at the end of the tunnel. I came to discover later there was no tunnel at the first place. I was alone in the middle of nowhere, cut off from human society that I know.

I never have stress as I trust God in every step that I take. I thank Lord, God Almighty for his care and protection. Within my five years in exile and counting, I got my second son and I named him, "Lion of Judah""Netanyahu" because God had made me conquer all the challenges, "Tong Nhialic" God's war. The first born was Awan, "Christo" I call him.

Good News Bible
Ezekiel 34:1 -10
The Shepherds of Israel

The LORD spoke to me. "Mortal man," he said, "denounce the rulers of Israel. Prophesy to them, and tell them what I, the Sovereign LORD, say to them: you are doomed, you shepherds of Israel! You take care of yourselves, but never tend the sheep. You drink the milk, wear clothes made from the wool, and kill and eat the finest sheep. But you never tend the sheep. You have not taken care of the weak ones, healed those that are sick, bandaged those that are hurt, brought back those that wandered off, or looked for those that were lost. instead, you treated them cruelly.

Because the sheep had no shepherd, they were scattered, and wild animals killed and ate them. So my sheep wandered over the hills and the mountains. They were scattered over the face of the earth, and no one looked for them or tried to find them. "Now, you shepherds, listen to what I, the LORD, am telling you. As surely as I am the Living God, you had better listen to me. My sheep have been attacked by wild animals that killed and ate them because there was no shepherd. My shepherds did not try to find the sheep. They were taking care of themselves and not the sheep. So listen to me, you shepherds. I, the Sovereign LORD, declare that I am your enemy. I will take my sheep away from you and never again will I let you take care only of yourselves. I will rescue my sheep from you and not let you eat them.

Good News Bible
Isaiah 48: 1-14
Zion the City of God

The LORD is great and is to be highly praised in the city of our God, on his sacred hill. Zion, the mountain of God, is high and beautiful; the city of the great king brings joy to all the world. God has shown that there is safety with him inside the fortresses of the city,

The kings gathered together and came to attack Mount Zion. But when they saw it, they were amazed; they were afraid and ran away. There they were seized with fear and anguish, like a woman about to bear a child, like ships tossing in a furious storm.

We have heard what God has done, and now we have seen it in the city of our God, the LORD Almighty; he will keep the city safe for ever.

Inside your Temple, O God, we think of your constant love. You are praised by people everywhere, and your fame extends over all the earth. You rule with justice; let the people of Zion be glad! You give right judgments; let there be joy in the cities of Judah!

People of God, walk around Zion and count the towers; take notice of the walls and examine the fortresses, so that you may tell the next generation:

"This God is our God for ever and ever: he will lead us for all time to come."

God's Will on the People

The shepherd that will lead South Sudan, I prophesied, will be a liberator, but a civilian who has been through the struggle and has seen it all. A son of South Sudan who only leave the country to seek knowledge and wisdom of God. Just like King David conquer other nations and return to the promise land of Israel and build the Capital Jerusalem. God promise him that his son Solomon will succeed him as King and he will rule with peace. God gave King Solomon wisdom and knowledge to rule his people with just. God promise that King Solomon will build the temple of God and he will rule with just, if he follows the rules that were given to the servant of God, Moses.

So, the next leader of South Sudan will be a witness of the liberation struggle and he will have no blood on his hand. He has not killed anyone in his life, so that he can do the work of God with peace and God's protection. God will give him peace on his reign and he will do what pleases God. Building the temple, leading the people to repent their sins and keeping the people united will be his mission and God will give him peace and prosperity.

God has preserved the leader of South Sudan; he has not witnessed the horror and the massacre and so, his mind is not spoilt with hatred and revenge. God is preparing a leader, someone who will bring peace. He should not rule with the picture of what happened to his people and so, he comes to revenge, to kill and continue the reign of war, rather, he will be a reconciliation to the people of South Sudan and rule with just and wisdom.

God will be with him and he will destroy all the household gods and idols that people worship. With the support of priests and the world prophets he will open "The Heaven's Gate" and break the ground for the building of the temple of God. All his ministers and civil servants will be people who worship the Living God of Israel, Living God of South Sudan and he will appoint pastors and men of God to advise him, rule the country.

The Living God of Abraham, Isaac and Jacob has not forgotten the people of South Sudan. The independence that the people of

South Sudan got was not from the blues, that is the fulfillment of the word of God that shade light on the people. Just like Israel, they endured suffering and discrimination in the hands of their enemies but God delivered them, gave them a country and made them courageous among their enemies. They lived to defend their families and their land. Today, Israel have made a name globally for the best Agriculture technology, water technology and their scientist have a global recognition supporting larger countries in Africa, Asia and Europe.

For the case of South Sudan, this independence marked the transition of God's nation and glory of God to reign on the land forever and with the nation building and peace to the families of South Sudanese. We have sinned against God and against His throne, we need to repent our sins and God will forgive us as a nation and we will be blessed and have a leader that unite us. Our grandfathers, our fathers and ourselves have sinned against God, we need to repent our sins as a nation and fast asking for forgiveness. To have a good leader, and to have peace in the country is a blessing that comes from God. As the saying goes, **"When God wants to judge a nation, He gives them wicked rulers" Jeremiah 23:19** we can confess that we have wronged God and that is why we do not have peace and a ruler to unite us.

God has given us a chance through his son Jesus Christ. Whoever repents through him will be forgiven and have a new life. We repent our sins and believe and have faith that the blood of Jesus will wash away our sins and now that we are clean, God bless us and make us prosperous in the land, to enjoy and be witness of your glory and preach the word of God. Amen.

Good News Bible
Isaiah 18: 1 -7
God will Punish Cush

Beyond the rivers of Ethiopia there is a land where the sound of wings is heard. From that land ambassadors come down the Nile in boats made of reeds. Go back home, swift messengers! Take a message back to your land divided by rivers, to your strong and powerful nation, to your tall and smooth-skinned people, who are feared all over the world.

Listen, everyone who lives on earth! Look for a signal flag to be raised on the tops of the mountains! Listen for the blowing of the bugle! The LORD said to me, "I will look down from heaven as quietly as the dew forms in the warm nights of harvest time, as serenely as the sun shines in the heat of the day. Before the grapes are gathered, when the blossoms have all fallen and the grapes are ripening, the enemy will destroy the Ethiopian as easily as a knife cuts branches from a vine. The corpses of their soldiers will be left exposed to the birds and the wild animals. In summer the birds will feed on them, and in winter, the animals.

A time is coming when the LORD Almighty will receive offerings from this land divided by rivers, this strong and powerful nation, this tall and smooth-skinned people, who are feared all over the world. They will come to Mount Zion, where the LORD Almighty is worshipped.

The Vision of the Bulls

As I was called rebel, by my fellow South Sudanese just because of having a contrary opinion with their views and the views of the

President of the Republic of South Sudan, I had to accept the name as I needed justice and equality to all South Sudanese. I needed peace and stability. I did not actually have a contrary opinion, my father did and I was accused and held responsible for my father's loyalty to the country. I was never recognized for his great achievement. Either was I praised for his contribution to the independence. I was not respected for my father's eleven bullets wound and his twenty-one years of struggle to get South Sudan's independence. I was not congratulated for the best military headquarters he built. I was not honored for the tallest building in Awiel he constructed for the party using his money. I was not appreciated for the first ever tarmac road he made in Awiel since the universe was created. I was not acknowledged of his achievement, but I carried the cross of his undefined dispute with the President. I am at the heart of being targeted, and killed for what I can't define, where the problem initiated at their place of work.

In order to hurt us, they named us rebels as the word opposition was soft and could not have been used to kill us. The word rebellion was dangerous and more violent and that would keep us permanently on the run and in exile, compared to opposition which could allow us to do our politics in the country.

The country was in chaos with over twenty rebel groups or political parties, all living in exile or in the bushes in the country. The witch-hunts of the government forces have forced many to abandon their ancestral homes and go to refugee camps. The government never honored any peace agreement and was ready to eliminate the rebellious groups and their leaders, civil societies and youth leaders. No one that was safe in South Sudan. From a mere student to a graduate who had skills to a business person who was supporting hundreds of people in the country, all are in the target list. The leadership was willing to eliminate potential youths, anyone with skills was dealt with severely, security personnel were ready to execute any order brutally.

One evening before I slept, I knelt down to pray to God. My concern was about my country, peace and the next leader that would unite us. I wanted to know and I wanted God to help me know the next ruler, next President of South Sudan among the opposition groups. I needed peace and I believed only God holds the keys to a peaceful and prosperous South Sudan.

"God please help me do the right thing. Help me to determine the future of South Sudan. Help me God to know who will bring peace and prosperity to the people of South Sudan. Whom has been chosen as the next President of South Sudan. God, I pray with faith, in faith and trust that you will answer my prayers in s vision, I prayed and believe. Amen."

The LORD Almighty answered my prayers same night with a vision. He gave me a vision that needed Spiritual leaders to interpret not based on my interest but the interest of the people of South Sudan.

In the Vision

"I was in a gathering of young South Sudanese warriors. They were armed with spears and clubs. In a distance, there were so many white bulls, tethered on a nail on the ground. We were angry youth seeking a solution to a persistence bullying by the bulls. As young warriors, we agreed to first kill the bull that was ahead of the rest of the bulls. We moved towards the bulls and we circled the first bull. I moved to my right while we circled the bull in front of other bulls.

The bulls were so many that I could not count them. What would happen to the rest was less important, our instincts were on the agreement that if we kill the first one the rest will vanish, or will be at our command. We moved and circled the first bull with our spears. I saw my colleagues throwing their spears to kill the first bull but none of the spears could pierce and kill the bull. Several warriors threw their spears trying to kill the bull but all was in vain. They bounced off, the bull was well fed or the kind of spears we had were weak compared to his strong skin.

The bull was well fed and his skin was strong for a spear to penetrate through.

I was losing hope and courage; I was also losing faith as well on killing the bull yet I had not thrown my spear to try my luck. In a wink of an eye, I saw the bull holding a spear that was bigger and stronger than the rest that we had and before I knew it, I was the target of the bull in the crowd of the youths that lined up to kill him. He threw his spear in an attempt to kill me. In the process of trying to escape the spear that was coming toward me with the muscle speed that threw it, I stepped on cow dung, slid and hit the ground, supporting myself with my hands.

The spear missed me, flied over and hit the ground a few yards after me. Beside me was an old hut, faded thatch hut old enough to leak. I turned to look where the spear of the bull had fallen, reached for it and gained confidence, hope and faith that I would kill the bull. What gave me confidence, is that I had a stronger spear that would kill the bull, his own spear. When I got up to my feet, I saw the bull had been wounded twice. One on his front, left leg and the other one on the front, right leg.

I had courage that I had seen where I was going to hit and kill the bull with one pierce to his heart. I began to move around seeking a space to kill the bull while I tried to get close to it"

I woke up from the vision.

Good News Bible
1 Kings 3:1-15
Solomon Prays for Wisdom

Solomon made an alliance with the king of Egypt by marrying his daughter. He brought her to live in David's City until he had finished building his palace, the Temple, and the wall around Jerusalem. A temple had not yet been built for the LORD, and so the people were still offering sacrifices at different altars. Solomon loved the LORD and followed the instructions of his father David, but he also slaughtered animals and offers them as sacrifices on various altars.

On one occasion, he went to Gibeon to offer sacrifices because that was where the most famous altar was. He had offered hundreds of burnt offering there in the past. That night the LORD appeared to him in a dream and asked him, "What would you like me to give you?"

Solomon answered, "You always showed great love for my father David, your servant, and he was good, loyal, and honest in his relations with you. And you have continued to show him your great and constant love by giving him a son who today rules in his place.

O LORD God, you have let me succeed my father as king, even though I am very young and don't know how to rule. Here I am among the people you have chosen to be your own, a people who are so many that they cannot be counted. So give me the wisdom I need to rule your people with justice and to know the difference between good and evil. Otherwise, how would I ever be able to rule this great people of your?"

The LORD was pleased that Solomon had asked for this, and so he said to him, "Because you have asked for the wisdom to rule justly, instead of long life for yourself or riches or the death of your enemies, I will do what you have asked. I will give you more wisdom and understanding than anyone has ever had before or will ever have again. I will also give you what you have not asked for: all your life you will have wealth and honor, more than that of any other king. And if you obey me and keep my laws and commands, as your father David did, I will give you a long life."

Solomon woke up and realized that God had spoken to him in the dream. Then he went to Jerusalem and stood in front of the LORD's Covenant Box and offered burnt offerings and fellowship offerings to the LORD. After that he gave a feast for all his officials.

Good News Bible
1 Kings 1:5-10
Adonijah Claims the Throne

Now that Absalom was dead, Adonijah, the son of David and Haggith, was the eldest surviving son. He was a very handsome man. David had never reprimanded him about anything, and he was ambitious to be king. He provided for himself chariots, horses, and an escort of 50 men. He talked with Joab (whose mother was Zeruiah) and with Abiathar the priest, and they agreed to support his cause. But Zadok the priest, Benaiah son of Jehoiada, Nathan the prophet, Shimei, Rei, and David's bodyguard were not on Adonijah's side.

One day Adonijah offered a sacrifice of sheep, bulls, and fattened calves at snake rock, near the spring of Enrogel. He invited the other sons of King David and the king's officials who were from Judah to come to this sacrificial feast, but he did not invite his half-brother Solomon or Nathan the prophet, or Benaiah, or the king's bodyguard.

Good News Bible
1 Kings 1: 11-52
Solomon is Made King

Then Nathan went to Bathsheba, Solomon's mother, and asked her, "Haven't you heard that Haggith's son Adonijah has made himself king? And King David doesn't know anything about it! If you want to save your life and the life of your son Solomon, I would advise you to go at once to King David and ask him, 'Your Majesty, didn't you solemnly promise me that my son Solomon would succeed you as king? How is it, then, that Adonijah has become king?'"

And Nathan added, "Then, while you are still talking with King David, I will come in and confirm your story."

So Bathsheba went to see the king in his bedroom. He was very old, and Abishag, the woman from Shunem, was taking care of him. Bathsheba bowed low before the king, and he asked, "what do you want?"

She answered, "Your Majesty, you made me a solemn promise in the name of the LORD your God that my son Solomon would be king after you. But Adonijah has already become king, and you don't know anything about it. He has offered a sacrifice of many bulls, sheep, and fattened calves, and he invited your sons, and Abiathar the priest, and Joab the commander of your army to the feast, but he did not invite your son Solomon. Your Majesty, all the people of Israel are looking to you to tell them who is to succeed you as king. If you don't, as soon as you are dead my son Solomon and I will be treated as traitors."

She was still speaking, when Nathan arrived at the palace. The king was told that the prophet was there, and Nathan went in and bowed low before the king. Then he said, "Your Majesty, have you announced that Adonijah would succeed you as king? This very day he has gone and offered a sacrifice of many bulls, sheep, and fattened calves. He invited all your sons, Joab the commander of your army, and Abiathar the priest, and just now they are feasting with him and shouting, 'Long live King Adonijah!'

But he did not invite me, sir, or Zadok the priest, or Benaiah, or Solomon. Did Your Majesty approve all this and not even tell your officials who is to succeed you as king?"

King David said, "Ask Bathsheba to come back in" – and she came and stood before him. Then he said to her, "I promise you by the Living LORD, who has rescued me from all my troubles, that today I will keep the promise I made to you in the name of the LORD, the God of Israel, that your son Solomon would succeed me as king."

Bathsheba bowed low and said, May my lord the king live forever!"

Then King David send Zadok, Nathan, and Benaiah. When they came in, he said to them, "Take my court officials with you; let my son Solomon ride my own mule, and escort him down to the spring of Gihon, where Zadok and Nathan are to anoint him as king of Israel. Then blow the trumpet and shout, 'Long live King Solomon!' Follow him back here when he comes to sit on my throne. He will succeed me as king, because he the one I have chosen to be the ruler of Israel and Judah."

"It shall be done." Answered Benaiah, "and may the LORD your God confirm it. As the LORD has been with Your Majesty, may he also be with Solomon, and make his reign even more prosperous than yours."

So Zadok, Nathan, Benaiah, and the royal bodyguard put Solomon on King David's mule, and escorted him to the spring of Gihon. Zadok took the container of olive oil which he had brought from the Tent of the LORD's presence, and anointed Solomon. They blew the trumpet, and all the people shouted, "Long live King

Solomon!" Then they all followed him back, shouting for joy and playing flutes, making enough noise to shake the ground.

As Adonijah and all his guests were finishing the feast, they heard the noise. And when Joab heard the trumpet, he asked, "What's the meaning of all that noise in the city?" Before he finished speaking, Jonathan, the son of the priest Abiathar arrived. "Come in," Adonijah said. "you are a good man – you must be bringing good news."

"I am afraid not," Jonathan answered. "His Majesty King David has made Solomon king. He sent Zadok, Nathan, Benaiah and the royal bodyguard to escort him. They made him ride on the king's mule, and Zadok and Nathan anointed him as king at the spring of Gihon. Then they went into the city, in an uproar. That's the noise you just heard. Solomon is now the king. What is more, the court officials went in to pay their respects to His Majesty King David, and said, 'May your God make Solomon even more famous than you, and may Solomon's reign be even more prosperous than yours. Then King David bowed in worship on his bed and prayed, 'Let us praise the LORD, the God of Israel, who has today made one of my descendants succeed me as king, and has let me live to see it!"

Then Adonijah's guests were afraid, and they all got up and left, each going his own way. Adonijah, in great fear of Solomon, went to the Tent of the LORD's presence and took hold of the corners of the altar. King Solomon was told that Adonijah was afraid of him and that he was holding on to the corners of the altar and said, "First I want King Solomon to swear to me that he will not have me put to death."

Solomon replied, "If he is loyal, not even a hair on his head will be touched, but if he is not, he will die."

King Solomon then sent for Adonijah and had him brought down from the altar. Adonijah went to the king and bowed low before him, and the king said to him, "You may go home."

Wisdom and Knowledge

We have learnt that the plans of LORD and his will, the God of Israel will always prevail. God showed Moses and Aaron the promise land and he showed us the promised land of the people of South Sudan and taking people there would be someone whom God has anointed just like King Solomon was anointed to succeed his father, King David. Moreover, when Adonijah claimed the throne and that was not the plan of God. God of Israel was able to humble him and he bowed down in front of King Solomon whom God had chosen to succeed King David.

In the vision of the bulls, God will rescue the people of South Sudan and he will give them a ruler like his servant King David. This person will be a God-fearing man and he will do what pleases the God of Israel, the Living God of South Sudan.

The people of South Sudan have had conflict for the last five decades and there has been vacuum in leadership, vacuum of spiritual leaders and vacuum of the word of God to be spread across the country. The liberators of the country did not have an opportunity to go to school, know Jesus and worship God. They were caught between traditional religion and Christianity. They needed that traditional rituals to encourage them fight the war and they needed Christianity to get support from Christians community in America, Israel and the rest of the Christians states. They needed military and food aids. That drove them to Christianity to get support from their Christians fellows and practiced their rituals to feed their egos and hoped they wouldn't be killed by the bullet. This is why the war took a turn to be a religious war and not political differences. The animist South Sudanese had to associate themselves with the religion that was accommodative to them.

In the struggle, there has been few Christian churches, hence attendance was smattering and the Gospel was never spread to all communities. The people did not have a specific place for settlement as they were a guerrilla movement. There was no church, as any tree could serve as a service and holy place to worship God.

Many still believe in their traditional beliefs and their traditional gods. The people of South Sudan need change and they needed to know God.

The few churches that have come to the city have not been able to reach the countryside and teach the locals in their native languages.

The people of South Sudan believe in their traditional gods and though that has not brought much impact, it's time to get a ruler that will lead them to worship the Living God of South Sudan, God of Israel.

People are craving to learn but there is little teaching as war has denied them the access to go to church. And many churches are located in the city denying those in the rural area to know God and learn the teachings of the bible.

A mother in the village of Aweil would be struggling to get food during a protracted dry summer, while her child treks for fifteen kilometers from home to school daily and when exhausted on this dry season walk to school, he drops out and his chances of knowing God are diminished.

A typical Nilotic mother would distribute the work force to her children while the husband would lazy in the shopping center, playing cards.

She would ask her son to go look after the goats while an elder boy would be asked to look after cattle. A young girl would be grinding sorghum and after finishing, she would go and collect firewood and light the fire for evening meal. She'd be going to fetch water at a well five kilometers away from home, come back and help her mother prepare the dinner.

The boys would have brought back the cattle and goats; the girls will have to milked them. If there is any little time available for the family, it will be story telling about the traditional norms and believes.

This has hindered the spread of the Gospel in South Sudan. We shall be grateful to have our people learn about the LORD, Jesus Christ. Learn about the plagues that happened to the children of Israel and how God stood with them.

They would be happy to read the bible and learn about the miracles and the world around them.

Today in South Sudan, the few churches that are available are in the cities and only those who do not have the intention to guide the Christians have come to confuse them more so those who do not know anything about Christ. The people in the city go back to seek rituals to succeed, get jobs, appointments and wealth. They have forgotten that God guides the universe and has power over all things.

There are many churches in the city then in the villages where majority lives.

We would like the government to regulate the churches as some of them are only misleading citizens and not bringing them to the LORD.

More Churches, Wider Spread of the Gospel

The more we have churches in the country of good and same denomination, the more the Lord will be present in our lives. All the churches need to be regulated to help the people of South Sudan to know God and not another scamp of misleading the country and the people of South Sudan. We all know how much a misguided religion in the country can lead us into unwarranted civil war. The failure to guide the religion in Sudan led us to war. We will not allow that to repeat to our children and the generation of South Sudan. If we set rules and create a good manifesto guided by religious leaders, we will be able to separate the religion and politics in the country.

The government and religious leaders to bring criteria to opening a church. Many people are not spiritually prepared and have not studied the bible. We need those who are spiritually prepared to guide us, and led by God's power to teach and preach the word of God. There are those gifted by the spirit to teach the word of God. We will always allow those gifted by the Holy Spirit. But more importantly, regulation of churches should be of importance in Christian manifesto, guided by the spiritual leaders.

Rules and regulations of starting a church will always be in the national manifesto of the Christian Coalition and South Sudan Society of Churches. Serving God should be a true calling and worshiping the Living God of South Sudan and a task of the spiritual leaders to lead the people of South Sudan on the right path to see the glory of God.

The church and politics must be separated and worshipping God is a duty and a good choice for all Christians and the people of South Sudan. The rights of Christians should be put forward by their spiritual leaders and must be on the national manifesto. Only on the manifesto will more rules and regulations be found. The national Christian manifesto will be developed by the spiritual leaders from the Christian fellowship and guidance of the Holy Spirit.

South Sudan will be open to invite and welcome world prophets, pastors and all religious leaders to support the people of South Sudan. Men and women of God all over the world will always be invited to help in prayers and groundbreaking for varies churches and communities place of worship. God will always be our beginning and ending of all events with respect to other human rights and our traditional norms of respects.

The spiritual leaders must and should help in abolishing the household gods and traditional worship and turn the people to God. Building churches and destruction of idols worship should be done by Christians leaders. As a secular state, there will be freedom of worship, freedom to choose your religion and freedom to worship your gods and God. All churches that will exist will only support one true God and that is the God of Israel, the Living God of Abraham, God of Isaac and God of Jacob, we will not allow anyone to mislead our people and cause **another civil war** in the country for the sake of religion differences. In the abolishment of idols and other gods, that will help the country establish herself and worship one true God.

Good News Bible
2 Kings 23: 24- 27
Other Changes Made by Josiah

In order to enforce the laws written in the book that the High Priest Hilkiah had found in the Temple, King Josiah removed from Jerusalem and the rest of Judah all the mediums and fortune tellers, and all the household gods, idols, and all other pagan objects of worship. There had never been a king like him before, who served the LORD with all his heard, mind and strength, obeying all the law of Moses; nor has there been a king like him since.

But the LORD's fierce anger had been aroused against Judah by what King Manasseh had done, and even now it did not die down. The LORD said, "I will do to Judah what I have done to Israel: I will banish the people of Judah from my sight, and I will reject Jerusalem, the city I chose, and the Temple, the place I said was where I should be worshipped.

Jesus Christ Appeared to Me, Year 2017

When I was in the defunct state government of South Sudan, I was blessed to have served as a State Minister of Agriculture and Forestry and again I served as minister for Education, Acting Minister for Health, Minister for Youth, Culture and Sport and Parliamentary Affairs. I believe that my appointment in Northern Bahr el Ghazal was not normal. Looking the nature of competition that I won the position, I came to conclude that God was with me. Northern Bahr el Ghazal was the most peaceful, most populated and with the highest competition for potential, creative and energetic youth in the country. Sleep and you'd be the laughing stoke of the community, so one had to be awake throughout to make a difference in his family, society and the country at large.

The criteria by which I got the appointment was unbelievable. I come from a typical Dinka family where opportunities were given according to the birth position and rights. God had a plan for me and my contribution was something to look at and my qualifications. The liberators were not ready to hand over power to the youths, but God knows the transition period and who will lead God's country, South Sudan.

If I say it was God, then that can happen as miracles are always from God. I just finished university and the youth of Northern Bahr el Ghazal unanimously agreed and wrote a letter to the Presidents and to the appointing governor that I should be a representative of the youth. Paramount Chiefs also wrote their letter and the letters were endorsed and I was appointed.

Of course, no one does not pray when they need or are expecting something good to come their way. I prayed. I never thought I would serve in the government that early. Serving at that age was shocking and unexpected. I trusted anything was possible before God.

As I worked in the states, I helped the youths realize their dreams and supported the women group and their cooperatives. As Agriculture minister, I supported the farmers' cooperatives and assisted the community with the available tractors and we did a fabulous work in the field of Agriculture. There was plenty of food and we eradicated food insecurity in my reign.

I was the first Minister who introduced Awiel Marathon in Northern Bahr el Ghazal. I did it when I served as the state Minister of Youth and Sports, in NBGs.

One morning, before I waking up, Jesus Christ appeared to me in a vision. I saw his face; I saw his wounded hands and his face was so close that I could feel his breath. He never spoke a word.

He left and I woke up only to find myself in my room and the sun was up and bright. I prayed and prepared to go to work as usual.

That was my first time in life to be in the spiritual realm. Jesus Christ, the Son of the Living God appeared to me in a vision. That was miraculous and I believe each one of us has a chance if we repent our sins. Jesus is willing to perform more miracles if we believe and follow His teachings.

I talk to my colleagues about the miracles and Jesus appearing to me, none took it seriously as it seemed impossible to none believers and that marked my spiritual realm journey. Angels later come to appear and more miracles happen that if it was not God with me. I wouldn't have survived the assassination attempts and the struggle. **I will always stand as a testimony for the Kingdom of God.**

I have always prayed to God for help to my people. As I served as a government minister, there were little resources and there was high demand from the public. One had to go to his own pocket to help the needy. The government did not have budget for all the services needed for the community. There were no jobs for the youths but we tried to create jobs while others had jobs with no pay. They had to wait for months before we could get budget increment so we could put them in payrolls.

What stood with us was God and only Him gave us hope and strength to live for another day. I vividly remember, there was a young man who had been coming to the ministry of Education for nearly three weeks looking for his three months' pay that he had not got. He was a teacher in one of the local schools in Awiel East. He walked fifty kilometers to and from his home to the ministry of education. His salary per month was only five dollars and he needed three months' salaries. The teacher had an issue with his name. The names he had in his identification had an error and did not match the names on the payroll. It had been addressed previously and it should not have been an issue, but now found it difficult to get his payment.

When the finance administrator brought the case to my office, as government minister for education and child welfares, I had to listen to him, though he has missed classes due to the delay in payment of three months' salary and his family was struggling. That showed me how much there was need for a better government that would deliver services to the people. There was need for salary increment for teachers and other government workers. And having little influence to direct the national government, I saw God as the solution to the problem. As a state minister, I brought the motion to the Council of Ministers, but little was done as the National Government was to reverse their budget then the states would be considered. I did not have authority on the budget of the state and laws that would serve the people well. I had to go into my pocket to get fifteen dollars and pay the teacher after I had proof that he was indeed a teacher. Many others are facing the same challenges and there is no one to listen to their cries.

The suffering of our people and lack of services was mental

torture to those leaders who were willing to help but had no means. Seeing them suffer and no capacity to support or rescue the needy was a psychological torture. Women delivering by the road side because hospitals are far from reach and there were no ambulances. Witnessing such great suffering in an independent country is a heart breaking to anyone who sees it.

When Jesus appeared to me, it gave me hope that there was a future to the people of South Sudan. God is watching and God would rescue them one day. I believe that God is the solution to the suffering people of South Sudan. The leadership has no regards to the common citizen, but God loves the people of South Sudan so much that, Christ died on the cross for their sake. I have a strong belief that God will appear to the people of South Sudan at the top of a mountain and the people of South Sudan will repent their sins and worship God and peace will come. God will give them a ruler that will bring peace and prosperity to the land, where all will walk and travel without fear.

Peace will come when they have an anointed ruler like the servant of God, King David. God will use his servant to unite the people of South Sudan and return those in exile and those in refugee camps. God will save the people of South Sudan just like He saved His own people, the children of Israel. The foundation of every country is God and Jesus is the lead. There is no country that is not founded by LORD, God Almighty. I believe the challenges facing South Sudan today are because the people have failed to follow the word of God and worship idols and household gods. When they turn to God they will be rescued. God rescue us not because we have changed but because, He is a God of mercy and has power to forgive and bless. Amen.

For anyone to be successful in South Sudan today, he or she must look for those who worship idols and the black magic. They do it to get appointments of government positions and the top leadership believe in it as well. This has affected the country and God that gave them independence has abandoned them to their gods and idols. A girl who want a good marriage must seek the traditional gods and idols that will confuse the man with money and power in order to marry her and she will control him. God has abandoned the people of South Sudan because of worshipping their household gods and idols.

South Sudan was saved by the Living God and the people of **South Sudan need to repent their sins at Mount Zion as it's written in Isaiah 18:1-7.** They will have their country back and there will be peace and unity. The struggle that our people are going through is lack of worshipping the Living God. And only Him that will give us a ruler that will unite us and deliver South Sudan to the promise land. We could see the land but we are not there yet. Just like the way Moses saw the land of Canaan and he never put his foot there. The people of South Sudan are not yet in the promise land, they will only be there when the LORD, God Almighty bless them and give them a leader like Joshua to settle them in the promise land.

South Sudan might have got independence but because of the sins of our ancestors and our own sins that we have not yet repented, we will have to be in the desert just like the children of Israel who stayed in the desert for forty years. Those who left Egypt and had sinned against the LORD, God Almighty, did not see the promised land. So, is it with the people of South Sudan, LORD, God Almighty has given us a country and if we do not repent our own sins and the sins of ancestors, we won't enjoy peace and prosperity of this land. Unless the people of South Sudan repent and turn to God and their sins will be forgiven and we will all be glad to enjoy the fruits of the land. God, we repent our sins and sins of our ancestors, forgive us Lord, and now that you have forgiven us, bless us and let us walk in your glory forever Lord, Lord bless our families and bless our land with peace and prosperity. Amen.

Good News Bible
Jeremiah 17:14-18
Jeremiah asks the LORD for Help

LORD, heal me and I will be completely well, rescue me and I will be perfectly safe. You are the one I praise! The people say to me, "Where are those threats the LORD made against us? Let him carry them out now!"

But, LORD, I never urged you to bring disaster on them, I did not wish a time of trouble on them. LORD, you know this; you know what I have said. Do not be a terror to me; you are my place of safety when trouble comes. Bring disgrace on those who persecute me, but spare me, LORD, fill them with terror, but do not terrify me. Bring disaster on them and break them to pieces.

Good News Bible
Romans 1:8-15
Prayers of Thanksgiving

First, I thank my God through Jesus Christ for all of you, because the whole world is hearing about your faith. God is my witness that what I say is true- the God whom I serve with all my heart by preaching the Good News about his son. God knows that I remember you every time I pray. I ask that God in his good will may at last make it possible for me to visit you now. For I want very much to see you, in order to share a spiritual blessing with you to make you strong.

What I mean is that both you and I will be helped at the same time, you by my faith and I by yours.

You must remember, my brothers and sisters, that many times I have planned to visit you, but something has always kept me from doing so. I want to win converts among you also, as I have among other Gentiles. For I have an obligation to all peoples, to the civilized and to the savage, to the educated and to the ignorant. So then, I am eager to preach the Good News to you also who live in Rome.

God Show Me Rebelling
Against the Government - 2003

At my tender age, my spirit was strong and all my wishes came true and it still happens till this day. My Guardian Angels are always close to implement what bangs in my mind and thoughts, it happens immediately. My instinct is very strong and my Lord is very close to me. What I want happens and if not I have to say, "**JESUS PLEASE DO NOT LET IT HAPPEN.**" Those words have saved me a lot of childish wish and destruction. I grew up craving to know God. My first time to know or hear the word of God was when I was in Ethiopia and there was chaos with the leadership of Magisto Mariam. My brothers, cousins and I went to a Catholic church nearby to help the priest pack his belonging, he was leaving for Europe. Ethiopia was in a total chaos and Magisto Mariam regime was coming to an end. That was my first time to step into a church compound, not inside the church. I felt something running down my spine, shivering and the body hair stood. I paid no attention, what fear could have clothed me on a bright day light. The priest called out for our help and we excitedly rushed to help him.

We helped the priest pack and in return, he gave us paper bags of white small bread, I thought they were biscuits. The priest called communions. Each one of us was given enough communions. But to me, they were some white biscuits that dissolved easily once in the mouth. We saw him close his eyes and bless them. He prayed for them and gave us as many as we could carry. We ate as we were hungry and little did we know that they were holy communions. That was the first time I heard about religion and Christ Jesus.

Other than communions, I got a gift that I live to cherish for the rest of my life. A Catholic sister gave me a statue of Holy Mary, and she said, "This is the mother of Christ Jesus, our Lord." I kept that with me and I slept with it, never wanted to lose it, not even my mother could keep it for me. I knew I had a story to tell my village people and my grandmother whom we left in the village when we left for Ethiopia.

I was nine years old and impressed with the work of God. I was so much interested to learn more about God and Jesus Christ who was also called the savior and son of God. There was no one to answer my questions. 'why savior Jesus the savior of mankind not saving us? Why the son of God was not coming to our rescue?" I was felt with excitement and I knew, our case was human and what God help was spiritual and not man made. My mind was actually young and could not think complexly.

I lost the statue after six months of trekking back to Bahr el Ghazal, we were still lost in the midst of Equatoria forest with uncounted enemy attacks and ambush. At one time, we were ambushed, only to find myself dragged into muddy water by my mother. In a minute, blood was oozing out of a young soldier in military uniform next to me. The young soldier still had courage to hold his gun peeped to see where the bullet was coming from. He covered us and he beckoned my mother to move and he covered us. He shot the enemy while we moved. He was twelve years old, I was three years younger than him. When we came back, we helped cleaned the wound of the young man. We got no medicines, we have to use herbs to heal him.

In that snare, everyone lost their belonging. I lost my statue in that conflict. I felt hurt, I had lost the only precious property I owned. I had neither cloths nor toys; all I owned was my life and the Mary statue.

When we got to Awiel East my home town. I had a chance to teach my friends who never went to Ethiopia about God and Jesus. I just came from abroad, all eyes on me like Tupac Shakur, American musician. The journey that took us three years walk with all the ambush, God saved us and brought us back home and I met my grandmother, Aluat Wuieu.

Then, again, constant Maram attacks were still occasionally operating. The Maram who came to raid our village never ceased. We were at constant attack and that interrupted the schools that were operating under trees. In school, I met a friend who claimed to be talking to God at a certain tree near their home. I was impressed and I followed him everywhere asking him what God says, what plan God had for us and we could consult our daily activities and demands. I later came to know that what he was doing was not the God I wanted and so we parted ways.

I was later on baptized by a Bishop that came to our village to preach the word of God. He was from Catholic domination. That marked my religious life that summer. He was probably from Italy as Italians were the only priests we encountered in the country. Priest Mazilario baptized me.

I went to church that was thirty kilometers from home to and fro. That was not far considering the word that I was so eager to know. I had seen God saving and leading me in my age and in my thoughts. I have never met any danger in my daylight or at night. LORD, the God Almighty has been with me in all the ambush and saved me from wild animals. When I was fourteen years old, I had an opportunity to come to Kenya for studies, abandoning my child soldier services in the military barrack that I was supposed to attend. It was mandatory to join the army if one is at the age at which he can carry a gun.

September was a life changing moment in my life. Wish all Septembers come like the September of 1998. I left my motherland, my family, my friends and relatives in search of knowledge. I came to a foreign land where I knew no one and started new life with new faces. There were Swahili speaking people, very short and strange, who spoke a very strange language. I had to learn their language in order to communicate with them. God was with me. I settled in Kapenguria, Kenya, with a family that had been introduced to me on my arrival. I started my school at standard three class the year after.

I was in class eight, in 2004. That year, I was to sit for my final class eight exams. It's a national examination done across the country. I had a vision 2004, July. My life was normal. I was preparing to sit for my end year examination and we were on second term when I had a vision.

In my vision, I was in the forest with my father, Paul Malong. He was wearing a short and boots. He asked me to follow him. I followed him barefooted. I followed him in the forest, he was running and ordered me to run behind him. I ran with caution not to be hurt by thorns.

Though I followed him, I never got hurt. I knew God has passed a message to me, and the message is what came to reveal itself in 2018 and now living on the vision.

After I finished my primary, high school and also cleared my university, I went back to South Sudan and after three years of no job and hard hassle, I had a chance to serve as a protocol officer in the ministry of Foreign Affairs and later a State Minister in different portfolio in Northern Bahr el Ghazal government and defunct Awiel East State.

When my father was relieved and pushed to rebel against his own government, I found myself having trouble with the same government that I was serving. I was pushed to join my father in exile. Again, I saw the vision that I followed my father and I never got hurt. I saw God walking me through all these troubles and saved me; He had a plan for me just like He has a plan for South Sudan and the people of South Sudan.

Two Angels Appeared to Me

While I was still in exile two Angels of God appeared to me in a dream and they asked me simple but important question. They did not sound to me like I should answer, what I needed in my life or that of my family. The questions hit me with concern for South Sudan, what I wanted for the people of South Sudan. Given such an opportunity and audience with God, I could not mess it up with personal needs. South Sudanese are in exile; I was in exile and the reason of being in exile is lack of peace and that comes with vacuum in rule of law and poor governance.

When the Angels of Almighty God ask me, **"What do you want?" I said, "PEACE" and that was my answer. Peace. The people of South Sudan needed peace and prosperity and unity will come along as long as there is peace.**

I met the Angels of God in an open bright and white place, I believe I was in heaven. We walked side by side to a prayer room. At the prayer room, I knelt down before the Heavenly Father. I worshipped Him, God Almighty. In the prayers chamber while I worshipped God, the Angels of The Holy God asked me to state what I want. In the prayers chamber, there was a glass between me and the two Angels that questioned me. It was more like a podium where one could go in a catholic church to repent their sins, that was made of glass and the light was very bright. The glass between us had a space where I could touch the Angels, if I needed to pass my hands through.

God has stood with me and my family while in exile. I do not work and I have no source of income but I trust God in all maneuvers He has always provided for me shelter, food and protected my family. My life has been in danger several times, but God has never given up on me, I also place my trust and hope on our Lord Jesus.

After the Angels asked me what I wanted and I said **'Peace,'** they left and I woke up from the dream. I knew I had been visited by Angels of God. I knew God would one day bring peace to the people of South Sudan, as that is what I asked God ALmighty. if I was to respond as a human being, copying King Solomon's statement would suit me, "I need wisdom and knowledge," but since I was in the spiritual realm, the wisdom that God had given to me made me answer it right and not my personal needs. Peace to the people of South Sudan was the priority. No one is happy in South Sudan and peace will bring hope to the people and they'd worship God as they get opportunity to repent their sins.

Asking God to give his people peace and a ruler that would bring peace and rule them with justice would be greater than my personal issues. I want the people of South Sudan to know God and the only way for them to know Him is having peace and repenting their sins and worshipping God. Peace will soon prevail and a ruler anointed by God, God willing.

With peace, comes wisdom and knowledge, with peace, comes justice and accountability, with peace comes love, hope and faith, with peace comes the love of God and worshipping of the LORD, God of South Sudan, God of Israel, with peace comes good ruler and protection of civilians, with peace comes the knowledge of God, with peace comes the Holy Spirit, with peace comes the power of

Jesus Christ. Peace is everything that a human being needs on this universe. Peace is health and good environment. Peace is the country and the people with ruler and democracy.

Good News Bible
Sirach 17:25-32
A Call to Repentance

Come to the LORD, and leave your sin behind. Pray sincerely that he will help you to live a better life. Return to the Most High and turn away from sin. Have an intense hatred for wickedness. Those who are alive can give thanks to the Lord, but can anyone in the world of the dead sing praise to the Most High? A person who is alive and well can sing the Lord's praises, but the dead, who no longer exist, have no way to give him thanks. How great is the Lord's merciful forgiveness of those who turn to him! But this is not the nature of human beings; not one of us is immortal. Nothing is brighter than the sun, but even the sun's light fails during an eclipse. How much easier it is for human thoughts to be eclipsed by the stars in the sky. Human beings? They are dust and ashes.

Good News Bible
Sirach 18:1-7
The Greatness of God

The Lord, who lives for ever, created the whole universe, and he alone is just. He guides the world with his hand, and everything obeys him. He is the King of all things, and his power separates what is holy from what is not. He has given no one enough power to describe what he has done, and no one can investigate it completely. Who can measure his Majestic power? Who can tell the whole story of his merciful actions? We cannot add to them; we cannot subtract from them. There is no way to comprehend the marvelous things the Lord has done. When we come to the end of that story, we have not even begun, we are simply at a loss for words.

Good News Bible
Acts 22:6-16
Paul Tells of his Conversion

As I was travelling and coming near Damascus, about midday a bright light from the sky flashed suddenly around me. I fell to the ground and heard a voice saying to me, "Saul, Saul! Why do you persecute me?" 'who are you, Lord?' I asked. 'I am Jesus of Nazareth, whom you persecute,' he said to me. The men with me saw the light, but did not hear the voice of the one who was speaking to me. I asked, 'What shall I do, Lord?' and the Lord said to me, 'Get up and go into Damascus, and there you will be told everything that God has determined for you to do.' I was blind because of the bright light, and so my companions took me by the hand and led me into Damascus.

"In that city was a man named Ananias, a religious man who obeyed our law and was highly respected by all the Jews Living there. He came to me, stood by me and said, 'Brother Saul, see again!' At that very moment I saw again and looked at him. He said, 'The God of our ancestors has chosen you to know his will, to see his righteous Servant, and to hear him speaking with his own voice.

For you will be a witness for him to tell everyone what you have seen and heard. And now, why wait any longer? Get up and be baptized and have your sins washed away by praying to him.'

Good News Bible
Psalms 79:1-13
A Prayer for the Nation's Deliverance

O God, the heathen have invaded your land. They have desecrated your holy Temple and left Jerusalem in ruins. They left the bodies of your people for the vultures, the bodies of your servants for wild animals to eat. They shed your people's blood like water; blood flowed like water all through Jerusalem, and no one was left to bury the dead. They surrounding nations insults us; they laugh at us and mock us.

LORD, will you be angry with us forever? Will your anger continue to burn like fire? Turn your anger on the nations that do not worship you, on the people who do not pray to you. For they have killed your people; they have ruined your country.

Do not punish us for the sins of our ancestors. We have lost all hope. Help us, O God, and save us; rescue us and forgive our sins for the sake of your own honor. Why should the nations ask us, "Where is your God?" Let us see you punish the nations for shedding the blood of your servants.

Listen to the groans of the prisoners, and by your great power free those who are condemned to die. Lord, pay the other nations back seven times for all the insults they have hurled at you.

Then we, your people, the sheep of your flock, will thank you forever and praise you for all time to come.

A Vision of Three Rules and Three Golds

I was in the midst of a well-planned forest and there was a clear road. The trees were well arranged and in order, with short grass under them, the breeze was welcoming. I was standing on the road, and the trees were tall, racing high up in the sky. The plantation was more of a man made, the space under the trees was clear and they were in line. The breeze was good and calming. The trees did not ground randomly and there was a respectful grass that calmed the soul and allowed the wind to blow without disturbance. There was nothing to block one's eyes from one end to the other.

I was standing there with the Lord Jesus. I could not see his face, he was above me. I was comfortable not to see his face. The face of the Lord is brighter; I could go blind if I raised my eyes to see him. Jesus communicated peacefully to me. He gave me instructions and I was comfortable to accept them. He was above me and he spoke to me. I was standing and I could feel the Holy Spirit around me.

He gave me a small piece of paper and he said, **"There are three rules in this paper, follow them and you will get anything you want in life."**

I took the piece of paper from JESUS CHRIST and put it in my jacket's pocket. The spirit above left and I walked down the road.

I walk down the road; I followed the path after I got the rules. In a short while, I came to the edge of the forest. I got out of the forest as I walked down the grassland savanna road. There was a small bushy grass that created a corner between the forest and the plain grass land. I came past the corner and after a few yards, **I saw three golds on the ground.**

I went straight to pick the golds. I picked the first one and extended my hand for the second one, when I picked the third gold, it vibrated in my hand. I drop it and I picked it again, this time, it vibrated and I felt like it was a snake without a head, and thinking of a snake, I woke up from the vision.

I came to realize that I was visited by our Lord Jesus, it's only Jesus that we can't see His face because of His Holiness. The children of Israel could not see Moses when the glory of God shone on him. So, I had a meeting with our Lord Jesus and he gave me rules. He told me what I should share with the people of South Sudan and the world.

God had given me three rules in the dream and also gave me three golds and one of the gold was bad, as it vibrated. Maybe I was supposed to pick it or I was not supposed to pick it, only God knows. God will bring the meaning someday. I woke up and prayed to God to interpret for me the vision.

All these happened after three days of fasting and on the third day after fasting, I had the vision. God spoke to all the prophets in the bible through dreams and I believe God was speaking to me. He wanted me to pass a message to His people and to encourage them through His words and wisdom he has given me. God bless you all children of God and people of South Sudan and Israeli.

Good News Bible
Isaiah 58: 1 -12
True Fasting

The LORD says, "Shout as loud as you can! Tell my people Israel about their sins! They worship me every day, claiming that they are eager to know my ways and obey my laws. They say they want me to give them just laws and that they take pleasure in worshipping me."

The people ask, "Why should we fast if the LORD never notices?" Why should we go without food if he pays no attention?"

The LORD says to them, "The truth is that at the same time as you fast, you pursue your own interests and oppress your workers. Your fasting makes you violent, and you quarrel and fight. Do you think this kind of fasting will make me listen to your prayers? When you fast, you make yourselves suffer; you bow your heads low like a blade of grass, and spread out sackcloth and ashes to lie on. Is that what you call fasting? Do you think I will be pleased with that?

"The kind of fasting I want is this: remove the chains off oppression and the yoke of injustice, and let the oppressed go free. Share your food with the hungry and open your homes to the homeless poor. Give clothes to those who have nothing to wear, and do not refuse to help your relatives.

'Then my favor will shine on you like the morning sun, and your wounds will be quickly healed. I will always be with you to save you; my presence will protect you on every side. When you pray, I will answer you. When you call to me, I will respond.

"If you put an end to oppression, to every gesture of contempt, and to every evil word; if you give food to the hungry and satisfy those who are in need, then the darkness around you will turn to the brightness of noon. And I will always guide you and satisfy you with good things.

I will keep you strong and well. You will be like a garden that has plenty of water, like a spring of water that never runs dry. Your people will rebuild what has long been ruins, building again on the old foundations. You will be known as the people who rebuilt the walls, who restored the ruined houses."

A Vision of Dr. John Garang de Mabior

Dr. John Garang is the founder and the leader of the Southern rebellion, Sudan's People Liberation Movement and Army. The movement that helped liberate the marginalized people of South

Sudan and brought independence in 2011 after referendum. The peace was signed in 2005 by Dr. John after twenty-one years of civil war, a peace deal was reached. Comprehensive Peace Agreement (CPA) was signed, and after twenty-one days, he crashes in a helicopter coming from Entebbe Uganda, where he visited President Yoweri Kaguto Museveni of the Republic of Uganda.

Dr. Mabior fought for liberation of South Sudan for twenty-one years before the peace deal was broken in Naivasha, Kenya. He led the rebel movement with support from various countries. Kenya and Ethiopia hosted the refugees. Ethiopia trained the first batch of the soldiers and they fought to liberate Upper Nile region and Equatoria. Cuba supported in military equipment and United States of America, Norway, Israel, Zimbabwe, South Africa, Nigeria and United Kingdom came with relief for the displaced persons. Dr. John Garang was among other liberators that sacrificed their youthful age to seek freedom and all rights to South Sudanese, he was with the likes of President Kiir Mayardit, Gen. Paul Malong, Gen. James Hoth, Gen. Awet Akot, Vice President Wani Igga, First Vice President Riek Machar, Gen. Santino Deng Wol and Gen. Peter Gatdet.

After the death of Dr. John Garang, the country was left in the hands of his colleagues who were in the struggle with him. After two years of independence celebration, his colleagues waged war over the power struggle and resources distribution. That war never had an end rather it keeps displacing thousands of people and hundreds of innocent mothers and children dead. South Sudanese are in exile and many find themselves in refugee camps while others meet their deaths. I found myself in exile among other young potential South Sudanese who could have been victims of national security brutality if we could not have deserted the country.

From Nairobi, Juba is just one hour and half flight away but I cannot put my foot there else I will be a dead meat. Many young youths who were not politicians went to exile and made a state enemy, because of their family backgrounds while others were chased out because of their potential to get better jobs. The potentials who should help rebuild the country are the target of the state security institutions. The government have targeted my family, my mother and all my siblings just because my father who was a military Chief of Staff fell out with the President. That has made me and my siblings run for exile and all our businesses blocked and private cars taken by the government officials. They sold even the farm produce. They closed our shops, sold the goods and took mangoes from the farm and sold. They ripped us dry. They didn't want to see any one of us alive, they killed my brother, a mere student who had never had any interest in politics; he was a football fun. A good goalkeeper of our time.

While I Was in Exile a Vision Came to Me One Night

"I was in a meeting, at Habesha Hotel hall, along the River Nile. The gathering was of a South Sudanese family. And before the meeting was concluded, there was a suggestion that we should all go out and collect honey and sesame, that would be our lunch after the meeting. I came out and at the car parking area, towards the gate there was someone seated on a chair and one chair was empty. When I got close, I found out that it was our late SPLM/A founder and the first vice president of Sudan under the liberation ceasefire, Dr. John Garang.

Dr. John Garang was sitting with his legs cross sunbathing, in the morning sun. I came and greeted him, he then asked me to sit on the next empty seat. There was one extra seat next to him. I was standing there with one of my cousins. When Dr. John asked me to sit, my instincts told me not to sit on the seat he asked me to. Either out of respect or the spiritual realm shared their spiritual knowledge with me. We agreed to sit with him, but I requested for another seat. There were children beside who were playing with a skipping rope. I called one of them and asked him to bring us two seats and he did. We took our positions and carefully listened to Dr. John Garang. He never spoke. We sat there looking at one another and no one broke the silence.

I had never met Dr. John Garang in person, I only saw him in pictures and if I had ever had a chance, may be when I was young in Ethiopia or when we were running in the midst of equatorial and at that tender age, I couldn't remember him. That was the first time to see him in the dream.

Good News Bible
1 Samuel 3:1-22
The LORD Appears to Samuel

In those days, when the boy Samuel was serving the LORD under the directions of Eli, there were very few messages from the LORD, and visions from him were quite rare. One night Eli, who was now almost blind, was sleeping in his own room; Samuel was sleeping in the sanctuary, where the sacred Covenant Box was. Before dawn, while the lamp was still burning, the LORD called Samuel. He answered, "Yes sir!" and ran to Eli and said, "You called me, and here I am."

But Eli answered, "I didn't call you; go back to bed." So Samuel went back to bed.

The LORD called Samuel again, the boy did not know that it was the LORD, because the LORD had never spoken to him before.

So he got up, went to Eli, and said, "You called me, and here I am."

Then Eli realized that it was the LORD who was calling the boy, so he said to him, "Go back to bed; and if he calls you again, say, 'Speak, LORD, your servant is listening.'" So Samuel went back to bed.

The LORD came and stood there, and called as he had before, "Samuel! Samuel!"

Samuel answered, "Speak, your servant is listening."

The LORD said to him, someday I am going to do something to the people of Israel that is so terrible that everyone who hears about it will be stunned. On that day I will carry out all my threats against Eli's family, from beginning to end. I have already told him that I am going to punish his family for ever because his sons have spoken evil things against me. Eli knew they were doing this, but he did not stop them. So I solemnly declare to the family of Eli that no sacrifice or offering will ever be able to remove the consequences of this terrible sin."

Samuel stayed in bed until morning; then he got up and opened the doors of the house of the LORD. He was afraid to tell Eli about the vision. Eli called him, "Samuel, my son!"

"Yes sir," answered Samuel.

"What did the LORD tell you?" Eli ASK. "Don't keep anything from me. God will punish you severely if you don't tell me everything he said." So Samuel told him everything; he did not keep anything back. Eli said, "He is the LORD; he will do whatever seems best to him."

As Samuel grew up, the LORD was with him and made everything that Samuel said come true. So all the people of Israel, from one end of the country to the other, knew that Samuel was indeed a prophet of the LORD. The LORD continued to reveal himself at Shiloh, where he had appeared to Samuel and had spoken to him. And when Samuel spoke, all Israel listened.

A Vision of Genocide

Jesus is the son of God; Jesus is the Messiah and through him we are able to go to Heaven and meet with God the Father. Our sins are forgiven if we have faith, love, hope, humble and humility to our LORD Jesus. God reveals what is hidden and shows it to the people he wants on this universe. We must be faithful and honest to our Lord in order for him to reveal what is hidden. Faith without action is dead as it's said in the bible and action without faith bears no fruits. As Christian we must have all those qualities to enable us bear fruit of heaven.

I knelt down to pray as was my daily routine before I slept. While I was deeply asleep, a vision came to me in the wee hours. I was disturbed with the vision that the LORD have shown me. I couldn't understand neither was I able to interpret it.

"It was the month of July, 2019. In the vision, my father was a leader of a group and he sent me ahead with his loyalists. When I was on the ground, a conflict erupted and the people who belonged to me, the people I was leading were being killed by our enemies. The killers were using swords, panga, daggers and all kinds of weapons that could kill.

I was in the midst of the people who were being killed. I survived by luck in all attempts. We found ourselves in the caves and our enemies came and fished us out killing some of us. In all these killings, I survive by the grace of God. It was a genocide in comparison with the Rwandan genocide. While still in the midst of the crisis, we ran and hid at the top of the mountain and a good number of us were killed there. I found myself again hiding with others in small bushes and they cleared the grass and killed many of my people, I was left alive.

All along there was this white man who was running with us

and hiding. When the enemy caught him, they let him go but the white man couldn't accept to go without us, even though he was freed. He felt like he was one of us and he deserved to be killed like us even though the enemy did not want to kill him. He wanted to face the challenges we faced, he wanted to live like us. He was truly our loyalist and one of us, even though he couldn't be killed, he supported us and we loved him around. He was wondering why he was never killed, and he would not stop hiding with us and sharing the pain with us. This time, they found him after clearing the bushes, they killed the rest of South Sudanese and he was let free again with me. I was there as well free and never got hurt. God knows how I escaped the cave, and the killings at the mountain top and the one at the bushes.

After I saw many being killed in the bush where I was hiding, I decided to climb a tree. I saw there was nowhere left now. There was a "thou" tree nearby and it had very few leaves but it was a tall tree. I went up with the knowledge that no one would see me, since the enemy was concentrating on the bushes.

While I was up, a spirit came to me and reminded me of a vision God gave me in 2004. **A dream within a dream.**

In 2004, I had a vision, I was running with my father in the forest. My father had boots and a short while I was barefooted and he asked me to follow him. I followed him but I never got hurt. He was running while I run behind him. That vision came to me in 2004. That is the vision that came to me while I was in another vision in 2019.

That vision came as a reminder that nothing would happen to me, just like nothing happened to me in that forest. It came to me while I was on top of the tree. I got courage and faith that nothing would happen to me as the Spirit of GOD had spoken of my safety. I got down the **thou** tree and as soon as I touched the ground, the war ended and there were no more killings. The was a complete peace that came and all our hearts were filled with forgiveness and love. God touches our hearts with forgiveness and love, then peace prevails in the land.

The peace came at once and people had love for each other and felt exhausted with the war and hatred. The exhaustion came as a result of God's forgiveness and I could see the killers passing next to the people they were killing and none asked the other. They accepted reconciliation without being asked to reconcile. The killer could not say "Here are the people we were killing, or the people being killed could not say, here are the people who were killing us, lets revenge."

They could pass each other without asking any question. There was complete peace and acceptance of coexistence.

I could see a person with a gun passing next to someone who has no gun and they could not ask each, I saw this outside at the fence. Each person went their way in search of means to survive and live. The society was busy in search of personal development and there was no hatred. I moved to the gate and I found young and disabled at a queue begging. Beside them was someone selling very small and sweet cakes. They were a size of ball gum. I had bundle of ten notes in my hand. I bought the cakes and I gave two people one cake to share. It was satisfying for those who took a piece. Whoever was given a piece of the cake got satisfied and never came back.

While I was distributing the cakes to the children, my dad arrived. I gave him the cakes I had bought and asked him to give it to the children at the queue. I took a few and crossed the road, to two other women who were begging across the road. I gave them the cakes and I could see excitement on their faces.

After I crossed the road and gave the women cakes, I woke up only to find out that God had been with me in the vision. God showed me what would happen in the future. I woke up and prayed and later shared the vision with family and friends. Since it was my first time that such had been showed to me, no one took it so serious, not even me took it so serious.

That month, I had several other visions including two Angels of God's visitation. I need peace for my people of South Sudan, because with peace, the word of GOD can be spread countrywide, with peace there would be love, faith and hope for the coming of the Kingdom of God. I saw peace come to those whom God is pleased with and they pleased God. That same month I saw the person whom God had sent to save the people of South Sudan. All these visions came but I never took them so serious. I thought they could be mere dreams. God had given me a message to the people of South Sudan, I came to believe and trust God that all that happened with the prophets in the bible can also happen today with us.

In the month of August same year of 2019, there was a war that took place in Awiel. They were soldiers coming from Meram, and they were seeking a place to settle in peace in South Sudan, as they seek peace with the government. They were loyal to the political party that I belonged and had a voice. Many of them were my relatives and brothers. These were not rebels, these were young men chased away by the Governor as he hated Malong, so he chased away Malong's relatives and friends. These were people so close to me and I knew them at a personal level. They fell into an ambush of the South Sudan military; many of them were killed under the order of the governor and division commander.

The killing was more selective and biased, those who were picked out and killed were people who were so close to me. All the people who were killed were more than one hundred. That killing remind me of the July genocide that I saw in a dream.

The death alarmed insecurity to all that came from Northern Bahr el Ghazal and Awiel East in particular. I shade tears for my brothers, relatives and friends that I lost in that ambush. That was a very hard moment to comprehend. The visions that LORD, GOD ALMIGHTY showed me were coming to reality. I prayed that all the visions especially the one for the genocide not to happen but God has all the reasons to make it a reality. I could not stop it from happening in any way. As I write this visions down and the word of God, I pray that God gives me a solution to all that He shown me. I have had more visions ever since that day and God has been kind and good to me on all that I do to spread the word of God.

The Serpent and the Black Panther

When the evil struggles to take the people of God, God always send his Holy Spirit to save and protect his beloved people. All people belong to God, only those that decided to do evil are lost sons and daughters of God and God is always willing to forgive and welcome them to His presence. One night while I was sleeping, the year 2020, the year of Covid-19, when all media was fully covered with Covid-19 news, I had a vision. The only hope people had was to turn to God. The technology and the experts had all been unsuccessful to find cure. The witchdoctors had surrendered and accepted that only God could save the world from such pandemic. The prophets and pastors saw the power of the Living God had come and the world was turning to God. Science could not find a solution to the infectious disease that was found in the air and killed instantly.

I was in the sitting room, standing behind the sofa and there was a lady standing on my left side. On the head rest of the seat was a serpent that had raised its head to see me. The cobra was furious and raised its head not to attack me but, kinder had a friendly gaze. Directly from the sitting room, I could see a black panther (Tiger) standing outside facing me in the house and looking at me directly.

Immediately, I got a question from the spirit asking me. **"Pick one among the two, serpent and black panther** I was left stranded and confuse. I don't know why I was to pick one and what will be safe with a human if I was to make a choice between the serpent and the black panther.

I was stranded there not knowing what to pick and what to do. I did not know what to pick and for what purpose. While I was stranded there looking at the tiger." I woke up and I found that I was dreaming.

Five months later and I had not made a choice. That lady left for South Sudan without telling me.

I prayed and thanked God for the gifts of the Holy Spirit and for the protection and always praying for my enemies to be safe and God to change their hearts for them to be my friends again. I prayed for peace in South Sudan, peace in Israel and peace in Kenya and United States.

Angels of Governance

The leadership starts at the personal responsibilities and how one leads themselves. The governance starts at the personal accountability and honesty. The self-love and care. From the personal level, the person becomes a member of the family and one is assigned with responsibilities and assignments by the family. That is where governance begins. **The head of the family decides what to be done in the family and sets rules and regulations.** Those are the norms and values that guide the family. The family comprises of the father and the mother, children become the welfare and continuation of that family where love and self-care is transferred. Each family works for the future and only for the future of children and generations after.

The family is unified with other families to make up a location, estate and the community that share certain norms and values. The families come together to make a community. In such a situation, there is need for the breakdown of norms and values, the community has to decide who will lead them and that becomes the head of that community. The chief or a chairman. As the father heads the family, the community decides who will be the head. Human beings in generations have found means to keep themselves and avoid extinction by setting rules. These rules help the weak not to be exploited and killed by the strong and the strong not to be mobbed by the weak.

The communities come together to make a nation and the nation sets its rules and votes in one person to guide the rules and regulations. A country can be headed by the president, king or prime minister. The set rules help nations, communities and families to exist and to continue the livelihood of the generations to come.

As nations comes together to make a continent and the continents make up our universe. Humans have tried to create unifying organizations that bring the world together, such as United Nations. Above all these unified nations and universe, there is God that sets rules and regulations. God rules all over the nations and universe; all creations bow down to God and worship Him.

The world is known to be one and is kept in existence by one power and that is the Power of Almighty God. The entire universe is under the care and protection of God. The governance starts from above and that is heaven. If we have head of a family, head of the nation all these are brought together by the power of God. God is the creator of good governance and human beings. All that we do comes from God and through God we learn to do good.

On the night of 22ⁿᵈ Friday in the month of May, 2020. as usual I prayed to God for peace in South Sudan and as the hour has come for the people of South Sudan to be given a good shepherd and peace.

I prayed, "God bless the people of South Sudan and gather them from countries they are scattered and bring them back to repent their sins and worship the Living God of Abraham, God of Isaac and God of Jacob in their promised land. Hallelujah, I praise you my God Almighty, I worship and glorify the true God of Israel, the God of South Sudan, the God of my ancestors, God of my father and the God of my mother." I worshiped God and slept in peace.

That night I had Angels of God's visitation. I met them in the Spiritual Realm. I met two Guardian Angels, **the Angels' of governance.** The Angels God have assigned in the department of governance to choose and guide all nations and those to be chosen as leaders. God have assigned them to watch over countries, I thought to myself, probably, **they were tasked to appoint, endorse and bring leaders that would rule countries according to the will of God.** Just as others are brought to power by evil spirits to come and kill and cause instability, so are the Angels of God assigned to bring right people to power and rule the people of God justly. Good leaders help in spread of the word of God and bring people to repent their sins in blood of our Lord Jesus the Messiah.

In my vision, one Angel was a woman and the other was a man. A sign that I should have the love of a mother and strength of a father.

The two angels told me in the Spiritual realm, I accepted their endorsement. They told me to leave the rest to them, and I would be called to the throne. The throne of heavenly assignment. Immediately they left and I woke up.

Then, the dream continued when I fell asleep again. I met another person again in the continuation of the dream, and this person only showed me the house of the people who endorsed me. He pointed at the tallest building among the buildings and he said, 'One of the people who endorsed you, live up there'. I tried to remember the names of those who endorsed me and I could not remember again in the continuation of the dream. I had a feeling I should go and thank them. We tried to walk to his house and I woke up as we walked there. I was going there to tell him thank you.

I pray to God and I worship Him forever for remembering the universe and his beloved people. I pray for peace and prosperity of the people of South Sudan. May God grant us peace, love to love one another and worship God, may we worship God and repent our sins and stay in our lands with no fear of insecurity. God, we trust in you. God our Father, give us a good shepherd to unite us and protect our properties and be prosperous in the land.

The Heavenly Realm is ruled by God who has put structures and departments to report to God our Father. The angels who are responsible for the governance of all the countries does God's will. The angels make sure that whoever God wants to rule a certain country will. They implement God's will.

Toothless Old-Looking Young Man

I had a vision, and in the vision, I was an owner of a new house with a broken lift next to the chimney. I walked to the living room and as I took two stairs off the living room to the reception and exit, a young man came from the broken lift and approached me. He came calmly and with politeness, he asked me to allow him to stay in my house. At the first glance, I realized he was toothless, young and strong looking man in his thirties. He looked strong with no teeth, making him too old, his lips collapsing inward.

At first I rejected his request. What came into my mind was, if my people would be safe if I lived with a stranger who had lost all his teeth and still looked young. This was a very strange human being and he wanted to stay in my house, the darkest part of the house, in the broken lift or chimney that had no lights. My mind was disturbed on what decision to make. He insisted that I should accommodate him. Due to his persuasion, I allowed him under one condition. I asked, 'I hope my people will be safe.' He said, 'your people will be safe.' He was very excited within seconds of saying yes. His mother came out from the broken lift. I guess she was listening to our conversation. She came out in a wheel chair, rolling it herself.

She was excited and with a smile on her face, she extended her hand to hug me, but I preferred to shake hands instead. She was also toothless. I was shocked. I shook her hand and welcomed them with African tea. I woke up while they were taking tea.

We need to pray that righteousness reign and we need to pray constantly and that we ask God to give us strength that Satan will not get his way in our watch and that we need to deliver our nation to serve God.

Quote from Kevin Zadai, "Every Christian should say, Satan will not operate in my watch and not in my presence, shut up and leave. There is nothing you can do about it, God has given me the key and I have power to send you away, go and leave. Amen."

God bless all the readers of this book. May whoever reads this book receive blessings and a breakthrough in their lives. May God bless this book to reach all Christians and children of God.

May whoever read this book receive blessing from God Almighty and Jesus Christ the Messiah and the son of God.

Topic Three:

The Slave Trade

Warawar as a Commercial Centre

WARAWAR IS AN ANCIENT TOWN of sub-clan of Dinka Malual, the Panchieny clan, Wun Anei people. The name Warawar was coined after the grandfather of Paul Malong Awan Anei Tong Agany, named after "Anei." 'Wun' is a sub-location predominantly occupied by one people who shared the same norms, values, beliefs and kept cattle together and are believed to be one people who can't inter-marry. Though it has existed throughout the colonial period, Warawar grew when the clan conflicts ceased and barter trade was spreading across Bahr el Ghazal.

'Warawar stands for, 'war' means river/swum while 'awar' means reeds. So, in Dinka translation, it's a swum of reeds or a river of reeds. People use reeds to make boats and mats. Reeds have a common usage in our society as they can also be used to make a house doors, boats, fishing basket or granary and bags for travels.

Warawar was a swamp area with reeds that were sold to various communities in the region. When Tong Agany opened the court as the Paramount chief of the Chiefdom, his court attracted many cases and many travelled distanced lands to come and appeal their cases. The common cases of Dinka were always rotating on marriages; someone took a daughter of someone and they did not pay dowry or theft of cattle which was not so common. The worst crimes to ever be reported were adulteries, a man found guilty was to be fined with seven cattle as the Dinka traditional law required, women were never accused of such acts even when found guilty. This was done to discourage men and scare them away from other men's wives or wife.

The justice that people got in Tong Agany courtyard brought many to Warawar and encouraged barter trade. The British and the Arabs were predominantly based in the North Sudan while the south was marginalized and left as a source of slaves. All those who appealed in Warawar courtyard got fair trial and they left pleased with the judgement.

The market grew as all the people who came needed food and accommodation. Tea was commonly taken in Mading Awiel thus its market grew rapidly. Then there was a demand for those who were fined to trade and get the cattle to bailed themselves. If there is one thing that Dinka has never constructed was, prison. Anyone who the court feared of his or her disappearance was taken to paramount chief's house to stay till the case is over. The chief took prisoners to his house, especially the minor cases of a girl that got pregnant or family dispute between a man and his wife. The search for bails, food and accommodation attracted people to Warawar and it grew simultaneously to be a commercial center of the people of Awiel East and Bahr el Ghazal.

The chiefdom was later inherited by Anei from Tong Agany who later named it after himself, 'Wun Anei.' When Anei passed on, he handed over the chiefdom to Paul Malong Awan in 1965's at a tender age. Through the family lineage, there has been no Christian name till Malong came to being and, him being named, Paul Malong seemed to have introduced the Christianity into the chiefdom. He is the first one in the family to have Christian name as introduced by missionaries during colonial period. The economic activities of Warawar were farming, cattle keeping then they embraced trading. They are predominantly Christians and animist, Dinka are never Muslims, the indifferences have put them into conflicts for decades.

Warawar became a commercial center that cattle, goats, sheep and grains flocked into the market from the region. Boys and girls would walk from Atok Thou and Gog Machar to buy goods and services, others would come from Gogrial to Warawar to buy 'nyarkub' a black plastic closed shoe for girls and cloths. The common cloths in the market were 'Jelabia' for men and 'jabon' (skirts) were sold for young girls and women.

As the center grew and goods and services were exchanged at affordable prices, it attracted the first Maram who came to sell salt to the locals. The Dinka called them, 'Jur awai' (Arab who came with salt). They came during Tong Agany reign when South Sudan was being encroached by both the Maram traders and the French who later handed over the colonization of South Sudan to the British during the Paris conference of 1800's.

As the locals traded with cattle, sorghum, goats and sheep, 'Jur Awai' came with salt and cloths from Meram. Warawar grew to be a commercial center in the remote area of Northern Bahr el Ghazal.

All the villages flocked to sell their goods and services in Warawar. Even though the center grew rapidly, there were no schools introduced, no hospitals and churches or mosque. As usual, the Maram worshipped anywhere and the paramount chief did not allow them to build their mosque in the area. The missionaries settled in Majok Akoon where the church was built, Christians had to walk twenty kilometers to church and another twenty kilometers back.

When Maram introduced their religion and culture to the locals, they found themselves welcomed to the chiefdom. It never took long before children were kidnapped and youth disappeared mysteriously.

Monday is always the market day of Warawar since time immemorial. One Monday as the people were busy selling and buying goods, it was always barter trade in those ancient times, the Arab raiders came to raid the market and they swept away all the youths and children leaving those who came to the market late and elderly. That was the beginning of the search for slave market and the hunt for slaves in Warawar in particular.

My father would tell me how he and his friends grew in fear of being sold or kidnapped by Maram slaves' hunters. The market that was growing became a den of hunt for slaves. They were taken to Khartoum and they found themselves overseas just like Bakhita was sold to Rome. This is the home town of Bakhita before she was taken to Nuba mountain where she was later sold again.

When I was born, I felt on the already existing problem and not an opportunity as there was no opportunity left in my village. I was born to the chiefdom of Wun Anei, to the mother Achol Kuel Athian of Pachier clan and father Malong of Pachieny clan both found in Wun Anei Chiefdom, under the leadership of paramount Anei Tong Agany. When I was born, there was a raid in Warawar and my mother had to run with me into the forest while I was hours old, my mother would always tell me this each time. This has been a story of decades, that I have to be told, when talking about Jesus Christ who had to flee to Egypt with her mother for safety, my mother has to compare her flee to the forest to that. She spent weeks in the cold hiding from Maram raiders.

I grew up in such a trying moment of hide and seek, anyone that was caught by Maram in Warawar market was sold in Meram, Khartoum and was never heard about. People did 'tol' (funeral) when they heard one of their family member had been kidnapped or had disappeared, they knew he would never return. We were scared with Maram and we grew up knowing them as evils, bad people and their religion allowed them to eat human meat. Many of our people were sold. I grew up in this environment, with no religion, no school and no hospital for the sick. Every day when we had nothing to do in the town of Warawar, we would move around with other youths counting houses that had been deserted, either they were kidnapped or they disappeared mysteriously in town.

Peace conference would be called by the paramount chief, my uncle whom my dad left the chiefdom to, when he joined the guerrilla war of attacking the Maram slaves' hunters. My father was based in Ang'ot with his soldiers, a village fifty kilometers north of Warawar. My mother was selling tea in Warawar town and we lived in Auchier estate just a kilometer north of Warawar central business center. My seven-year-old mind was always worried, that we are on the road towards the kidnappers and while my mother was in the market and my father away fighting the kidnappers and the government forces, we could easily be a target on the road to Warawar.

The Maram traders were spies who came to do slave trade and they would go with children whenever they go back to get more stocks in Meram or Khartoum. They did not accept this accusation whenever there was a conference to question the disappearance of children in town and the surrounding villages. With the authorization of the Khartoum regime that had accepted the slave trade in the country, selling children in the market was never a crime as long as they were not from Warawar, while the children from my village were sold in another market. Meram.

Children were brought from various villages and mostly Christian believers and were sold at a cheaper price, a price of a goat in Warawar. Up to date, in Warawar children are still scared with words like, "I will sell you to Maram if you do not work hard in school." That remained a scary story to be told by people today.

During a summer in 1991, the Sudan People's Liberation Movement/Army was coming to a collapse and the government forces were getting strong fishing out the guerilla forces out of their military base in the South. That year, there was a massive raid that took over five hundred children and youths in Warawar and in nearby villages. That raid left the people of South Sudan and the movement weak to apprehend. There was no home that was not affected and no family that was not crying for their child. Lucky were those who joined child-soldier a year earlier. That encouraged the remaining few to join the guerilla warfare and fight for independence. Children volunteered to serve in the war, and avoid kidnapping and slave trade.

All these continued as they were sold to work as slaves in Maram's homes and farms in North Sudan. For the few of us who were kidnapped that summer, we were sold three times on the way before we reached Khartoum. The raiders were hunters who raided villages and towns in search for children to recruit in their militia, others sold in the forest as merchandise to other businessmen who came from Meram. There was an open market a hundred and twenty kilometers north of Warawar. In this market, only Maram traders that met here, those who came from Warawar brought their goods here, which were kidnapped children. While the traders from Meram came with salt, cloths and sugar to sell to the locals in Warawar, these Maram who came to Warawar were the outlaw who escaped prisons or other crimes and so they lived their lives in the South and supported their families with slave trade.

Young men who could not walk for these hundred and twenty kilometers were killed. We witnessed the brutality when two young boys and three girls were slaughters on our watch. After this butchering, we all got energy and the journey was more like we just started a new journey. None of us wanted to die. They called us, 'jenge' meaning a primitive Christian. We were led by men with horses and other men on horses were behind us, there was nowhere to escape and with their cocked guns, death was close if one made any mistake. They never wasted their bullets, they only slaughtered whoever did a mistake. In my life, I had only seen a goat being slaughtered, and I had never slaughtered a chicken which was always a job for young boys in my culture. There I was, witnessing human beings, being slaughtered like chicken and they cleaned their knives on the dead body.

We were all scared to die, we did as they wanted us to, even if we were to kill ourselves, we would willingly accept and not die of that sharp knife. As we grew up in a Christian society of Warawar, we knew if someone slapped you on one cheek, you'd turn the other cheek, but here we were with no option of where to turn but rather die and not sure if Heaven would actually welcome us, Christians killed by pagans. All these happened when we were close to be baptized, we had missed to repent our sins and get cleansed. We missed our childhood life, education and the peace of being in our sweet home of Warawar and now Heaven and the word of God had been denied of us by Maram militia. What a painful death we would have had in the world of pagan, I thought. Many of us could have died of heart attack than the actual knife. I never saw these Maram brothers praying, I wondered if they really do.

When we got to the forest market of Maram where the traders would exchange their goods and services; those who came from Warawar got their goods and those who picked the slaves to Meram would pick their choices with the price tag of a goat as the highest for a strong young boy. I was sold with a price of half a goat, that means, two of us were sold as one goat, we were both young and not strong. There was this Maram who covered his face completely and only his eyes could be seen. He was the richest; he was allowed to pick first. He bought the weak us, and a few strong boys and girls. We were cheaper than those who were strong. This was the time, one wished he or she was not eating well at their homes so that they could be sold cheaply and never had to be given hard work. The protein, nutrition and energy from a village boy was being wasted by people who never fed not even one mouth among us.

It was not our choice to be weak, our genes were strong even though we looked thin. To our advantage, we were put on a cart pulled by a horse and we headed into a forest, literally, there was no caravan but we couldn't question. A slave had no rights especially a Christian slave in a Maram territory. Any complain met a beating or death. We quietly travelled in the dense forest, on the second day we had only been allowed to drink water and no food. If we were not carried by the cart, many of us would have collapsed and died of hunger, and still there were some who fainted in the cart.

On the third day, we were given 'hesh' (bread) with 'piu' (water) and kept in a forest. We did not actually know what was happening. We were told to be quite and wait for orders. The rest of the Marm were told to stay in a distance of one and half kilometers and the one whom we thought was the boss was left with us with one bodyguard. He had still covered his face and only the eyes were seen. After we had our 'hesh' and 'piu' we looked around and there was murmuring, some of the elder boys had already known the forest. We were back home. But why would a Maram bring us back home, we could not understand the logic. No one that had been kidnapped ever returned. "Are we being sold back to our families?" One boy asked. Jesus could have listen to our pledge and saved the first generation to know Christ and religion. We the 1980's and 1990's children.

As we waited to know our fate, then a lady came, whom we later came to know as "Lady Cock" we could not understand until later why she was named Lady Cock, but she was really a cock, I saw SPLM/A leaders honor her and the Maram who brought us bow down to her. We were sold back to our own people. We saw money exchange hands and we were told in front of the community that had just come to 'riangkou' (field) to identify their child and children to get to their parents. The kind of slave trade that was happening in Warawar was a nasty one. Those who were sold to other slave masters never came back. They were taken to Meram, Khartoum and sold further to Egypt and other worlds and countries that needed slaves. The few of us who were sold back were lucky to narrate the slavery trade in Warawar.

I vividly remember that we were kept for five days before we met our parents or guardians. The Maram who bought us and returned us was doing a trade of reuniting the children with their families on a fee. When there were no children recently kidnapped, he would get to Meram or Khartoum to buy slaves and bring them to Warawar and sell them back to the firm that was called, "Lady Cock". At our tender age, we did not know if that was the name of the organization or the name of the woman who used to buy back the slaves.

On the day of our reunion, we were given money, I got ten thousand Birr, the currency in Sudan those years of the struggle. As the slave trade ended in Warawar, many Maram found it profitable to bring their slaves back to Warawar and sell them back to their families. That nearly brought back another trade of young people being stolen and sold back to their families. Since only one person was authorized to bring back the children, that kept us safe, those who got back to their families' safely. I came to understand why, the Maram covered his face, he never wanted to be identified by his Maram colleagues as the one who abolished the slave trade and brought back the South Sudanese to Warawar and reunited them with their families. Teng Bol now eighty-three years old narrated me the story.

Persecution of Christians' Children

South Sudan is founded under the political indifferences that have lost millions of lives.

Tang son of Akon and his mother Abuk, woke up in the morning to go and milk goats, his mother Abuk and his father Akon left for the farm to cultivate. It was about nine o'clock in the morning when he woke up. Tang is from Patek clan of Awiel East county, in South Sudan. when he was milking the second goat in the goats' hut, he heard a blast in his compound and when he came to see, he was met with a slap on his face and he fell down. He was dragged outside and chained with other children and adults.

When he woke up, he was in a pool of blood. He cried softly as he had no energy and the voice could not come out. He touched himself to find where the blood was soaring out but he was not hurt. He was in a pool of blood of his maternal uncle who had been shot on the chest and died instantly from the bullet shot. They were chained in the compound and the anti-Christians moved around the village searching for more people to be captured and taken to be sold.

There were two men caught carrying two sacks of peppers and they were arrested with their sacks, chained together and they were also in the compound. Tang's home had become the center of the attackers where everyone was kept before they left for Merram. Abuk and Akon, Tang's father and mother was nowhere to be seen, probably killed or they might have escaped from the garden, Tang thought to himself.

After the anti - Christians had searched the entire village and captured all potential youths, children and killed the elderly who could not walk or can't do any work as they came to look for slaves. They came back to Tang's compound where other soldiers were left to take care of the prisoners. They came to divide the slaves and moved them to the market where many would be sold and others enslaved in the farms.

The two young men who were caught with sacks of pepper were asked what they do and they said they did business between Warawar and Merram and they were taking their goods to Merram market. They were asked, "you sell pepper to Maram, why can't you eat it here with your people, we will farm our own pepper." One soldier said.

Another soldier said, "Open the sack and start eating or we will kill you, we do not need competition with Christians in the market."

They were forced to eat the pepper. No water and no food each had to finish his sack. It was either they eat or get slaughtered. They ate until they fainted and they were left half dead. One of the survivors narrated the story in 1998 when the Christians came to save the people of South Sudan, the "Lady Cock" programed. His mouth had turned red, the hair on his head never grow strong and black as before. The pepper had weakened his immune system. His partner died after one week from the effect of the pepper.

Tang' was unchained from the dead uncle who he had been

chained with for two hours as the anti-Christians divided the people and cooked before they started their journey. The enemy was free to operate slowly as the South Sudanese Christians did not have any reinforcement, an organized army, moreover, it was the government that was raiding the civilians. They left hours later. After twelve hours of walking, those who could not walk any further were unchained from the group, both their hands cut off, and freed, they would never be a threat to the raiders. They thought.

The act gave Tang more energy and accepted to walk as there was no mercy to those who were unable to walk. They reached Meram in the evening of the third day. They were taken to a prison made of thorns, where they spent their night. Next morning, they were divided into two and the young ones were taken to the market to be sold while the elder ones were taken to the farm. Tang was sold to a Maram merchandize who took him to Omdurman and he worked there as a shepherd. He slept with the goats and he never had a meal unless it was a leftover from the table of his boss. He worked there for three years, he got beating daily either as a correction for a mistake or just making fun of him. He would be made to act as a dog, the family would go to the playground with him, then they would kick four balls and Tang was to run and pick the balls and bring them.

He was mistreated and cut with knife instead of beating correction. Thrice, he had been taken to the hospital in a critical condition and he survived them. One day he planned an escape with the neighbor slave who was also going through the same treatment. At that time, they would go to the farm to collect watermelons, that would be the best time. They went there once a week to get enough for the week for the family and market. They planned to leave the following week after Ramathan, when everyone would be busy celebrating and families visiting their relatives. There would be no one to watch over the slaves.

At dawn, they took a bus to Meram that was two hours' drive by bus. They arrived early as they escaped before noon. Meram was better as there were many Christians who were there. Some had escaped from their masters while others were those who came voluntarily due to famine and drought in the South Sudan. Others came in search of opportunities. So, Meram was more homily. There were no jobs to do for many Christians unless they accepted to work at the anti-Christians farmers who would enslave them, eventually. There were no rights for any Christians in that town. The anti-Christians made decisions and implemented them as it pleased them.

Tang and Quel, the other slave that escaped with him became homeless in Meram. The money they took with them was running out, if they couldn't find a job, the wouldn't survive in this competitive capitalist market. Going home, south was impossible. Many had died trying to go to south. They had heard all the tales of those who had escaped and tried to go back south and how they met their fate in the hands of brutal anti-Christians and wild animals. They were young and unexperienced; they voluntarily accepted to be taken in by a Maram businessman who found them sleeping outside his shop. He knew they might have escaped their master. He took them as his slaves. He took them to his watermelon farm to work and get free meals and a place to sleep in return.

They were made to join other slaves in the farm, they would work the whole day and couldn't eat not even watermelon from the farm. The bullet meal that came in the evening was only to keep them alive and continue working. The master was making thousands of Dinars and there was no payment on such hard work. Many escaped and more were brought and those who escaped met their death in the process. Tang grew up in the farm with his friend Quel and then they planned to escape and search for another work in town, though the only available jobs for slaves were well known. Its either a work in the farm, a shepherd or work as a waiter in a restaurant.

They succeeded to escape and they came to roam in town looking for a job. They could not find any decent job to do in the town. They decided to work in restaurants as waiters and did their savings. Months later, they opened a small four seats restaurants for their fellow Christians who were looking for local food. They operated the restaurant for six months successfully until someone went and reported them to the authority. Little did they know that Christians were not allowed to open restaurants in this town. If they could have gone to Khartoum, and opened it in Christian estates, it could survive but not on Maram area, where all restaurants are closed on Friday and during prayers hours. The Christians restaurant was open throughout and that brought a very stiff competition.

They were arrested by the police who took them to prison without trial. In the prison, they met others who had been there for months. One was tightened with a rope, two were tightened together at the elbows till the rope made the blood clod and rot, hence, cutting the hand off. Many who left the prison after their arms had rotten were later cut off. Tang was sobbing the whole day and night; food was thrown in the prison and they had to eat like dogs with their mouths, arms still tight behind their back.

It took a month for Tang to completely lose one of his arms and he was released to go and hustle with one arm. He spent months begging from his Christians brothers. No slave master would take him; he could not work efficiently as demanded. When some youth defected, and joined the rebellion in South Sudan, Tang joined them and he came back to his village. He never found his father and his mother, but home was better and safer than foreign land. He got married and he had four children that assisted him. His wife Atong was another girl who lost both his parents in her presence in one of the previous attacks. They both lived traumatized with the conflicted environment they were raising their children. She was hiding in the okra garden when her parents were shot in the compound. She had been surviving in the community, thanks to the paramount chief who took her in and raised her as his own.

They got married and they became a companion and an example of the generation of hope to the community that is still struggling. The persecution of the Christians had been witnessed by all the South Sudanese at all levels and this was just one case in thousands who died unrecorded and those who were still looking for their parents after abduction. Each year, thousands were killed and hundreds of thousands abducted by Maram and enslaved in Khartoum and other towns in the North. The abduction of Christians by anti-Christians has been there since independence in 1956 and that led to another rebellion and the secession of South Sudan in 2011. This abduction culture has made so many children in Bor community, Murlei and Nuer lose their children among themselves.

Hundreds of children have been abducted and never see their parents, the culture needs the current government and state government to investigate and create awareness, civil education and enlighten the communities to stop such practices. Awiel community alone has lost over half a million to abduction by Maram. As slavery has come to an end, let's try to create initiatives that create reconciliation and peace among the communities that were fighting the government agenda. Peace between Dinka Malual and Misyria is very important for our children to coexist in peace and harmony.

Peace between Nuer, Bor and Murlei is vital for their survival in the capital society, peace between Boya and Toposa, among other communities in South Sudan for a better and prosperous homeland.

Persecution of Christians' Women

Aman is a young girl from Warawar from the clan of Pachieny who was raised by her parents, Sultan Awan Tem and Aluat Geng in the village of Majak-Ajuong. She had never stepped at the doors of a classroom. She only went to the market on market-day to mingle and buy food stuffs and come back home. Their family was well-off, they had twenty cattle, thirty goats and fifteen sheep. Food was available throughout the seasons, when other families starved with no food in July, the only month between the new harvest and the old stocks and the food is always shortage. They had a farm for sorghum, sesames and groundnuts. Life was paradise to the little Aman. In the family roles distributions, she was tasked to fetch water at the nearby wells and collect firewood for cooking with her friends.

Her mother was a typical Dinka woman who made her homestead a typical Dinka home with, "kaal hook, and Luak" (that is a fenced compound for cows and a big hut for cows.) her mother had been "hooth' lower teeth removed, a transition moment from childhood to adulthood. She did that when she became a teenage, a year before her marriage. Aluat's family was the envy of the community because of her hard work and loyalty to her husband who was vying for the community chairman.

The wells were a distance from home and so girls had to go in a group and with the company of other young men. The young men carried spears, daggers and any weapon for self-defense. The water wells had been a hunting place for Maram abductors where a few lonely and criminals Maram would come to hunt. Also as a part of the culture, the youth used the hours of going to fetch water as a dating point. They got to find their loved ones and lucky ones got married and united the two clans that had been brought together by the young girl and the boy.

One day while the young Aman had gone to fetch water with her girlfriends, Abuk's boyfriend was there with other young men. They were to chat after fetching water before they go back home. The Maram abductors came in no seconds and shot the guns up to frighten the young men. They were already surrounded with men with guns, their spears and daggers could not do anything at that moment. The Maram captured all the twenty-two young Christians of Majak Ajuong area. Four young Dinka boys were killed and the rest chained and taken as captives.

Abuk saw her boyfriend Makuei killed in front of her and she was taken as a slave. They were taken to Meram and sold as merchandize. All the girls were raped in the forest before they were taken, and they killed those boys who tried to stop the rapists.

Girls were introduced to brothels and they became sex workers to rich Maram. There were Maram who did not want girls but wanted to sodomize the boys. They come to buy boys in the market. Abuk was enslaved and raped several times that she could no longer give birth when she came back to Malualkon when the Christians came to buy off the slaves and return them back to their homes, an initiative led by "LADY COCK."

Abuk was brought to Malualkon and since she could not give birth, she opened an orphanage to help raise the lost boys and girls who came back and they could not find their parents. The foundation is still in Malualkon today as Amandit Foundation, named after Amandit, the lady who saved several children and families in Awiel in 1988 famine. The abducted children of South Sudan who were taken by anti-Christians are fed and hosted by the foundation and with the support from good Samaritans and well-wishers, they get their education within the foundation premises.

Many women have faced rape and sodomize young men have been sodomized and those who resist were killed. The women of

South Sudan have suffered beyond measure. They are used for science test by those who have no knowledge of education. They were slaughtered as the Maram in that region mostly used knives. Many women have been operated through their private parts and left to bleed to death. There was a young woman who was to have her first born and she was left with only a month to deliver. She was operated under a tree and the baby removed as she cried her lungs out. She was later killed as her husband watched, then the husband's both hands were cut off and left to go and tell the story to those who would not accept to change their religion from animist.

There was another case of seven men with their wives, whom their wives were raped and they said they had to kill their men and one man was heard telling his wife, "Ask them if they can sodomize us and let us live instead" it was a mind torture, a very hard moment to bear and the hardest time to have been born, raised and living in Awiel, Nothern Bahr el Ghazal.

The women were raped and their men left alive.

I vividly remember, the man who asked to be sodomized, has never raised his voice in his family or discussed anything with his wife. The wife has used the statement to shut him up. Whenever this man quarreled with his wife in the village, the wife would say,

"Why am I being beaten with another woman who gave himself to Maram when disaster came."

This later forced the husband to later join the rebellion to fight Maram and stop the inhuman mistreat and sodomizing young Christian men in South Sudan.

There were many other reasons that let young Christians join the fight and seek freedom from the anti-Christian Northerners. Others left because their villages were raided and nothing was left to hold on in the village. Those join because of dredging of River Nile, which they did not want to be done. Nile is the livelihood of the people of South Sudan, they do not want the water to be sold out or dredge the river and lose their swarms and their rice irrigations scheme.

There was no life in the village. People were either in the forest hiding or farming; rainy seasons were breaks from raiders.

Others joined the rebellion because they never want to join any religion by force, as it was a forced religion and not by choice that they choose their faith.

Challenges of Churches and Christians

South Sudanese are Christians by birth, by blessing and luck of being colonized by British and by God's choice. Majority of South Sudanese are Catholic by virtue of it being the first church to have a structure in the ten States and they have strong faith in this church. Many of us are born Catholic just because our parents who were fighting the anti-Christians were Catholic and we had no education or knowledge and no strong faith or any spiritual attachment to the other churches. Due to this uneducated faith, our people stood a chance of changing their religion when they were exposed to know other religions that might lead them to the anti-Christians, religious extremist or guide their faith to terrorism. There is need of religion leaders to create awareness to the population and the missionaries to be given resources, time and space to give the accurate message of God to the people. The world is changing and our people need good guidance to make right choices in faith and in the families' future.

Such failure on the faith could arise through various social educations that would mislead the people who have no knowledge of the Christian faith they follow. As many are said to be Christians, they retreat to their traditional religious beliefs after attending church service. Such people are serving two masters and their strong faith is still on their tradition religion and not the Christianity they associate themselves. Christianity is taken by the people of South Sudan as a civilization institution and not faith based on one's goal to go to heaven after end time and believe in Christ Jesus as the Messiah. Rather, they take it as a social institution, they have to attend the church not to learn but to be associating with such institutions. We need more religious leaders to preach and access roads to the villages to spread the word of God.

The contribution of such challenges is the political instability, moreover, the spiritual leaders are not able to travel across the country, to the villages to preach the word of God. The political instability has made the word of God impossible to be spread in the countryside. South Sudan has had five decades of instability. The struggle between the north and south has made it impossible for pastors to go to towns that were under rebels or under the government to spread the word, as even the pastors were divided on political line. The government would not allow rebel pastors to preach in towns, they risk being killed and vice versa.

The politics played a role in the denial of South Sudanese to open churches and have modern structures. Many of these were conducted under trees and those that were better were the thatched huts which had to be constructed each year. The under-tree churches were never attended during rainy season due to bad weather and many are in the farm cultivating.

The churches are always facing financial crisis; hence, the pastors always depend on their farms and that makes them to take the work of God as a part-time job. There is no much commitment by those spiritual leaders as they have to spend their times looking for food and not studying the bible and preparing for the mass. The poverty in the country has made it impossible for the churches to grow. Many pastors face poverty and what the people offer to the church either a quarter kilogram of maize, or a quarter kilogram of floor and many do not come with offering. Such do not add to the development of church as the offering is used by the pastors to build the church and maintain the church services. The support of the orphans and widows is always done by the church through the offerings and support of the church members.

The poverty has stopped the growth of churches in South Sudan, many churches do not have branches in the rural areas. Those open in the rural areas are also not found in towns. This has affected the spread of the faith in the country. A person who is in the rural area will have to look for faith in a new church when he gets to town and a pastor or anyone who goes to the village will have to attend a new church as the church he goes to is not in the village. Moreover, not all villages are lucky to have a church and those that have churches will have to choose one young man to led them as a pastor which in many cases is always a standard three school dropout that would lead them in reading the Bible.

There is a high demand for churches and there are no enough resources to deliver such to the people. Poverty and instability have limited the spread of faith in South Sudan.

The South Sudanese are traditional religion believers and they have not been taught to understand the faith of Christianity. They turn to their traditional religion when faced with disaster and their faith tested. Many families live on less than 1.25 Dollars (one US dollar) per day. Hundreds of people die of hunger and malaria each year. This has made a church to be an aid organization that support the government to provide education, healthcare and nurturing the traditional families that are supposed to attend churches. The church creates awareness about the democracy and human rights and teaches less on faith as the people need to first know themselves.

The fundamentalism has flourished illegal arms trade and misled the traditional religious belief now turned into Christians into a radical Maram, confusing the locals even more on making the decision on religion. The conflict border of Maran and South Sudanese in Warguet and other borders in South Sudan and with endemic poverty will open doors to the brutal expansion of Maram and that could cause another war in the future. The churches need to be taken to such places and people's faith be strengthened as they are confused in the growing world and when they abandon their traditional religion they might find themselves in radical Maram and that would increase insecurity in the border and in the region.

The current political chaos could be another breeding ground for radicalism and they could be creating their bases just like it did in Somalia, the Al-Shaabab and the Boko Haram of Nigeria. South Sudan just got out from religious indifferences and having another religion conflict will destroy the fundamental existence of the country. The missionaries used to open schools to the community but the churches of today do not support communities with schools due to poverty and little faith of the Christians members to stand with the church.

The people have been forced to join the military and many soldiers do not go to church. The military commanders should be religious enough to encourage churches to be built in military barracks and all law enforcement institutions. This is because of the high unemployment that has given birth to crime, corruption which is causing more destruction than the religions conflict.

Again, the people have got out of religion conflict and found themselves in ethnic conflict that is widely spread in the country dismantling the fabric of the society. The common morality in the culture and religion is that they both believe that morality and values are through God, though they think that the western movies, culture of dress of the western world music and television have hurt moral standards of the people.

Majority of the people in South Sudan being traditional religious believers, turn to their rituals and traditional marriages either before the church wedding or after the church wedding. That makes it difficult for the churches to grow in the country. The people invest a lot in seeking the rituals and traditional blessing then seeking the glory of God and the message from the pastors. Any misfortune is believed to be traditional gods and idols that are annoyed and they seek solutions through household gods and not in churches. The have their traditional priest that consult gods on their behalf.

The marrying of many wives which is not allowed in the bible is a common culture and the people will not want to leave even though they go to church. They leave all that they have learnt in the church and come to follow their traditional lifestyles after church, and that has affected the spread of the Gospel in the country. It also discourages pastors especially those with little faith, who are under training with no experience. The notion that the religion is only left in church and the pastors while the people seek solutions in their household gods, has denied the spread of faith to the countryside. This has always been the culture in Africa and it would take great Spiritual leaders and a good leader to guide the people of South Sudan to learn and accept the Living God.

The modernization and urbanization has helped reduce the African religion in various countries and now they follow Christianity. South Sudan will need to develop and create opportunities to the population and Christianity will be accepted as they learn the modern way. Accepting Christianity and not following the Christians way of life does not make you a good Christian. They all say they are Christians but the influence of the tradition religion is too much and that is what needs to be wiped out and the country will be a Christian state as that is what the people fought to have.

The major teachings of Christianity includes:

1. The love of God with all your soul and with all your mind, love one another as you love yourself.
2. Love your neighbor as you love yourself, prosperity comes with love and Unity
3. Christians should be in one God; God is the solution and the answer to the mankind needs
4. Christians believe in Jesus Christ as son of God, the Messiah, Divine and human
5. Love your enemies, as you love yourself
6. They believe in the Holy Trinity, three in one, God the Father, God the son and God the Holy Spirit
7. The salvation of God can be attained by gracing the faith, love and humility in Christ Jesus
8. Forgiveness of sins and guidance of the Holy Spirit
9. The Bible as the source of Christian wisdom and life
10. The Christians belief in the second coming of Jesus Christ at the end time

Challenges of Pastors

Pastors do not have homes where they can live peacefully with their families as they preach the word of God. They lack food and basic needs as their job is to preach and there is no salary and source of income. They only depend on the good will of the believers who offer what their heart desire to give to God. They lack other social activities as they are a role model and so their integrity is their daily image of their followers.

The Sabbath Day

All Christians believe that God rested on the seventh day, and seventh day is Sabbath day and Sabbath day is the last day of the working day of God, according to various Christians and historians.

According to the bible, **Genesis 2:2-3**

"By the seventh day God finished what he had been doing and stopped working. He blessed the seventh day and set it apart as a special day, because by that day he had completed his creation and stopped working. And that is how the universe was created."

We have all read and confirmed the seventh day, but the question remains, what is the day that God rested? Many scholars have argued that the seventh day which is called the Sabbath is Saturday while the catholic have confirmed it as Sunday. In history, Sunday is said to be the day of the Sun. The early believers are said to have believed on the Sun and that is why the day was set for the sun to be worshipped which is Sunday, and Sunday was said to be the first day of the week and Saturday as the last day which is Sabbath day.

It's still not yet clear to many scholars and Christians which day is the last day at which God rested. In the bible, they only mention, God rested on the seventh day and on the count in the week, no one knows the day, and Israelis worship God on Saturday as they believe that it's the day God rest. Other Christians worship on Saturday while majority led by Catholic worship on Sunday.

Considering that the early Christians have said that Sunday was set as a day to worship the sun, and that made the Sunday, I can argue that Sabbath is Saturday and that is the day God rested and He asked, that all Christians rest on that day and never to work or travel. Jesus in his teaching he worships in synagogue according to the Jews and Moses's laws, but he never mentions Saturday or Sunday. He teaches about Sabbath day and glory of God. The

Sabbath day is not defined in the Bible and so it's hard for any scholar to decide on which day the Sabbath day falls. I can't decide either but I can shade light on it and the Glory of our Lord Jesus Christ will help us know the day and define it.

Muslims as we all know worship on Friday, we both believe in the same God and only differ on Jesus whom the Christians say to be the son of God and Muslims say, Jesus was one of the prophets. They worship on Friday as the seventh day that God took rest. The day at which God rested is not clear to many believers as each pick the day that suit them and according to their beliefs. As Christians of South Sudan, they need to find the Sabbath day with the guidance of Spiritual leaders.

The nation with its rulers, Spiritual leaders can always consult and find the Sabbath day to help find day God rested. The following of the rest day of God comes with blessing and glory of our God.

For many years, Christians around the world have not been able to understand and know the truth about the Sabbath day. Pastors only accept and go to theology and come and follow the culture and the norms that exist

Families of the Liberators

The survival of South Sudan in the geo-political and its socio-economy is vital as the survival of each and individual citizen of South Sudan in this era. God will be our light, way and the true guidance of our lives and our beloved country.

As good Christians, we need to remember families of all those who sacrificed their lives to liberate this country, the common soldiers whose sons or daughters needs basic needs, the widow stranded in the street and staring at hunger daily and need of clean water.

All South Sudanese families sacrificed their family members for peace and prosperity of this blessed and beautiful country. If a family had not given forth the father or mother to fight for liberation; then, a son or a daughter was donated to the liberation. And if one of the family member was not holding a gun then, there would be one holding a pen as a tool of liberation. Other families gave whole heartedly all they had, sons, daughters, father and mother and we lost them all, only memories of them that are left with us. It's upon us to remember such family lineage that have been wiped out by the conflict.

The people of South Sudan contributed equally and shed blood and later ended the five decades' civil war with a referendum. Referendum could not have come, if arms were not taken to make them hear us. The enemy we had listened more to the barrel of the gun than the word of mouth. Alas, they accepted our identity, our religion, culture, way of life and our existence in the region.

The families that could not join the liberation were given-up to the United Nations to protect. Our neighbors in the region hosted many of our refugees and educated them for the future. They got the refuge and protection, those who were left in the country in various villages in the country have been seeking survival in wilderness, caves and hills.

After referendum and independence, families came back from hiding to celebrate the independence. The government created institutions that had not existed in South Sudan since creation of the world. The economic cluster, service cluster and security cluster that will provide services to the newly crowned citizens of South Sudan.

When civil war erupted, it sent many into various refugee camps in the region and beyond. Those that did hide and seek with the enemy came back easily and resettled in the country. Those that left the country for refugee camps in 1980's, those that joined them in

1990's and those who recently went due to the 2013 political unrest are stranded and have no means to come back home. The camps are given food ratio and with no source of income, families, orphans and widows have no means to come back to the country. Moreover, starting a new life after they have come is another traumatizing thought for a single parent or orphan.

They read on newspapers and watch on news broadcast that war has ended in their country, but they need support from the government, United Nations or the international community and friends of South Sudan to put their hands together and help return the people of South Sudan home, and help them start a new life in their new environment.

The families of the liberators are stranded in camps. They lack transportation, the United Nations ratio is not sending them to grave neither is it fattening them. They are only surviving with the wish to go back home. The transportation, funds to start a new life in the new environment has proved to be beyond their thoughts.

The husbands and mothers, sons and daughters whom they offered to the liberation are dead, the young ones that they sent to refugee camps have grown, now they can't come back to their liberated country. They are forgotten in the camps. Either to celebrate their liberated country or cry over their loved one, they are traumatized in camps with no food, shelter and medication. Going to South Sudan has become a nightmare to comprehend.

The people who supported them have abandoned them since they heard the country got independent. Their sponsors have left them to fend for their lives in a society that they had never tried to hunt. The horror they live with is terrifying and it needs government intervention with the stockholders, the friends of South Sudan and people of good-will to rescue them. The families of the liberators need help to resettle back in the country with a better living standard.

The liberation period did not give us equal opportunities in education, talent nurturing and peace of mind.

A few got education while others were in frontline fighting for freedom, others saw the horror of the civil war while others were in refugee camps. We now need to offer equal services to all either educated or not with consideration that, they are families of the liberators. The liberators and families of liberators need support as much as we need to correct and strengthen our government institutions. We will not grow if we do not consider our citizens and all inhabitants of South Sudan equally and protect our territories and resources.

Creating **"Families of the Liberators Initiative"** can be a forum to support those orphans, widows and liberators that can't do any job in the society, those who are traumatized and the aged who cannot do anything or find an opportunity and have no dependent. Many youths, children and women are stranded in various refugee camps and wish to come back to South Sudan and they cannot afford to reach home. This should be an initiative to reunite families and rebuild the devastated country. An initiative to give hope and assimilate them into the society and give them value and dignity in the society. Restore hope and faith in the leadership.

The families need support and the "Families of the Liberators' Initiative" should be the voice to the voiceless families, orphans and widows in refugee camps, identify them and bring them to South Sudan for reunion with their lost liberators. Those who can join the orphanage in the country can always be taken, and those who can find their families can reunite. South Sudan's peace is not complete until all the people of South Sudan are resettled in their ancestral homes, and reunion is done with the Spirit and God of South Sudan. The natural world needs to reunite with the spiritual world. The disconnection has brought more problems and no settlement in our daily lives and the spirit are not settle either.

The widows and orphans are in refugee camps crying day and night for relief food, the ratio is never adequate. With the lack of adequate food, shelter and endanger of diseases, education has become an option for our children, not a priority. Now that we are blessed with peace, a country of our own, let's stand for our people and bring them home to worship God in our promised land.

If we are all citizens of the world, and we are citizens of South Sudan, let's remember that we are all liberators. The refugees call for the attention of International community while those who hold guns calls for the attention of the government. The two groups brought referendum and the liberators and the refugees voted equally bringing an independent nation. Their votes were counted equally and the results gave us an independent nation. The liberators who survived the horrific civil war that claimed two million lives in horrific situation today. While our mothers, children who were called, 'the seeds of the nation' are still in refugee camps where their fallen fathers and mothers, brothers and sisters sent them to refuge.

It's time that we remember our people in refugee camps and have an initiative to bring them back to the country. God that brought peace to South Sudan will bless the leadership that will bring back the scattered people of South Sudan around the world. The people of South Sudan need to repent their sins in the promised land and worship their God in the land that God has given them. The return of the people of South Sudan from exile should be an initiative of the church, government of South Sudan and all the people of good-will, the Families of the Liberators' Initiative and friends of South Sudan. God will bless whoever participated in this initiative, to support the people of South Sudan, worship God of South Sudan, God will have already been done.

Sid Roth's 'It's Supernatural!'

Side Roth is a Jew. The real names of the famous Sid Roth, the inspirational Jewish follower of Jesus Christ is, **Sydney Abraham Rothbaum**. He was born on 7th September 1940. He was born by Jewish parents. He is based in America and holds both Israeli and American citizenship. He said, "I was raised as a traditional synagogue where I attended bar mitzvah"

As he lived in America as Jew, he found organized religion irrelevant, being a Christian was boring but he was proud to be Jewish. As a young man growing up in America, money was all he wanted, his goal was to become a millionaire at the age of 30, graduate at the age of 29 and marry. He was a father to one daughter. Sid Roth was the account executive for Merrill Lynch. He had a good career and wonderful life, but he felt as a failure because he was not a millionaire at the age he targeted.

In Search of happiness, he left his wife, daughter and Merrill Lynch. His search led him to Eastern Meditation, the New age. He nearly lost his mind and life proved to be difficult.

At the age of 32 he converted to Messianic Judaism after a co-worker convinced him that Jesus was indeed the promised Messiah. The miracles and supernatural experiences confirmed to him after conversion that Jesus is the Messiah. He began his radio series Messianic vision in 1977. And his television show Sid Roth's It's Supernatural! Began airing in 1996.

In the late 2013, Sid Roth's had launched the "It's Supernatural! Network," a fulltime online network that streamed episodes of Sid Roth's It's Supernatural!

Each week, Sid Roth interviewed people who had experienced **miracles** and personal encounters with God. Some of the guests featured in Sid Roth include:

- Kathryn Kuhlman
- Kevin Zadai
- Jonathan Cahn author of The Harbinger
- Guillermo Maldonado, senior pastor of El Rey Jesus

How I Got to Know Sid Roth's 'It's Supernatural!'

I discovered Sid Roth's It's Supernatural! While I was searching on YouTube. I was wondering trying to know God better. I have read the bible and repeatedly gone through it. I have learnt the history of Israel, how God sent Joseph to Egypt and later his brothers and the father followed him. That marked the beginning of the tribes and the nation of Israel. The land was promised to Abraham but they had to grow in number somewhere to become a nation before they claimed their promised land.

I have learnt about Jesus Christ as the Messiah and the son of God. He was crucified and raised again so that our sins might be forgiven and that we will be born again by the blood of Jesus Christ. I got the helper was sent to guide us, lead us and protect us and the helper was the Holy Spirit. After I had read all these, I was thirsty for more knowledge about the Kingdom of God. That took me to the internet to find what will amaze me, shock me and question myself, if all these is not God, who else would it be?

My thirst to know God brought me to the amazing channel of Sid Roth's It's Supernatural! I did not know if that is the page I need to follow; I unknowingly subscribed to the channel at night while I was half asleep, I was not sure if I did it or my angel did it on my behalf. I watched several videos about angels of God appearing to people and I was amazed if all these were real and I wanted to google more and get to understand the world beyond education and the civil war that I have grew up knowing. The miraculous world was shocking and my curiosity to know beyond the bible and universe kept me awake till two in the morning.

I came across Kathryn Kuhlman and how she healed the sick, she was powerful that her surrounding was filled with realm of God that whoever got there fell down and got healed. Sid Roth was one amazing person whom all the people of God came to showcase their miracles. Roth's show was the center of my universe, I could get all the prophets, pastors and all those who follow Christ like me meet. I got blessed and my life changed from the day I watched videos of Sid Roth with Kathryn Kuhlman, Kevin Zadai and all the people whom God had sent to share the word of Christ with us.

Kathryn Kuhlman has helped so many people, blessed so many and brought many to Christ. She is a great woman that has mentored many Christians. I am pleased and blessed to write her names on my book. Kathryn Kuhlman. God bless Kathryn Kuhlman and her ministry that she has helped us to know the Lord, Jesus. God bless Sid Roth for a platform that made us learn more about the mission and miracles of God that have been shown to us in visions and dreams. Sid Roth has brought us together as children of God. Such reunion in Christ Jesus are a great blessing in our lives.

I have been recommending Sid Roth's Show to all the people of South Sudan and all Christians I meet. As it has changed my life, I am sure that whoever will watch it will have angels' visitations and he or she will be healed and learn more about the word of God.

What shocked me most and it has never left my mind is that "Pentagon" is ruled by angels headed by Chief Angel Michael. The angels ruled America for two reasons. One, that the American government continue to protect the interest of the people of Israel and safeguard them. Two, that the Americans to continue supporting and sponsoring the missionaries around the world for the word of God to reach to every nation. All these was confessed by Kevin

Zadai who several times has spoken to Angels of God. He said on the show of 'It's Supernatural!' that, angels gave him a book written in Heaven and he was told, when the time is right, then he will put his names on the book and reveal the secret of God to all nations. Kevin Zadai is a man who faithfully followed Christ Jesus and because of his faith in Christ, he prayed and worshipped the Living God and God had mercy on his ministry and angels of God were sent to guide him as he teaches the word of God.

If there is any television show that can change your life and receive supernatural experience, it is Sid Roth's It' Supernatural! This is the best television show that has changed my life and found myself writing a "Christian life experience and struggle in South Sudan." I recommend it to all Christians and those who wonder how the world comes to be, God is waiting for you with answers on this show.

Kevin Zadai is a prophetic follower of our Lord Jesus Christ. He has met with Jesus Christ in real life and he has had five and a half hours face to face meeting with our Lord Jesus Christ. He has been told about the change in the world and that all the suffering of the people does not come from God but from the enemy of Christ's followers. Satan wants to take the children of God away but Jesus has promised that the time for the "five wise virgins" has come and the people of God will do miracles. Through the messaged passed on by Prophet, a Messenger of our Lord Jesus, Kevin Zadai, said Jesus will be visiting his people at night in dreams and when they wake up they will be different people who will preach the word of God. Jesus said all to be ready and have oil in their lamps in their hand and be ready. Jesus promised to be with us and he will give us all that we ask for. During the day people, will preach the word of God and at night they will be having visitation from the Lord and these will be common believers not pastors. A time is coming when

God will be portrayed as a good God and all that happened will be to fulfil the will of our Lord Jesus.

The political unrest in South Sudan and like in any other country is not actually politics, it's Satan that is causing chaos to the believers. Satan is about to be defeated and so he is causing the war against the people of God. This is the time for the people of God to shine, they should not be silent as God will be with them and God's angels will guide them and protect them. The war about righteousness and justice is a war wage by Satan against the believers. This is the demons fighting back because they are about to lose their stronghold in South Sudan and the spirit of God will deliver the people of South Sudan and God's word will be preached across the country and to all nations.

"Truly I tell you, whatever you bind on earth will be bound in heaven, and whatever you lose on earth will be lost in heaven." Mathew 18:18

There is going to be a worldwide shortage of commodities and all the believers of God need to be ready and support one another. Our God, our Father is a good God and Jesus Christ is the answer and the way and it will last through Christmas. God's people will be protected as God did during the plague in Egypt. So, the Project Goshen is in effect. God protected the children of Israel and He is going to apply again in the world today. The people who believe in our Father God Jesus will be protected as God's plague in Egypt never spread in Goshen. God said to Kevin Zadai, tell people to repent and I will hear them from heaven and I will answer their prayers. Sid Roth added a quote, if more than two people sit and agree touching one thing in Jesus name it will be done.

Jesus told Kevin Zadai to tell the Christians, they are doing better than they think they are. Jesus Christ is encouraging us that our prayers are being heard and that we are doing well even with all these troubles and challenges that we face every day. Jesus sent a message that he has not rejected us, he loves us all his believers and we are doing better. Everybody is called to do his work in his track way that God has called us to do. Jesus wants all the Christians to stand up and continue preaching the word of God, they are doing better.

Satan is coming through the government that are not God fearing leaders. The government is collecting data on human and using it for Satanic deeds, so Jesus Christ told Kevin Zadai to give his electronic gadgets some break. God is advising us not to use the technology all the times as we need to pray and focus on the word of God. Satan is using the wrong leaders to revive old diseases and find means to spread it faster and easily. Give your electronic vacation every now and then. Lord Jesus said but if you all pray we can cut this off, all these do not happen in the world of our Lord, Satan is concocting new disease and reviving old diseases to fight the people of God.

Satan is using China to fight America and now there is another dangerous disease worse than covid-19 and God told America, according to Kevid Zadai, not to look for weapons or warship the war needs prayers and medicines not guns and bullets. Satan knows whom they don't want to get into the office as that leader that follow the word of God will revolutionize the system and word of God will be preached to all people. As they do not want President Trump in office as Trump is God's chosen leader that will do what pleases God. Kevin Zadai argue that Christians need to pray for a better justice system. Christians to pray for Attorney General and all the judges. If justice system is good, all the evil that have been hidden will be revealed and all that was hidden will come to surface. Those we never expect to go to jail will go to jail and people will have peace. This will expose all the magic and Satanic work of the leaders that rule us.

People will have to pray and say, "no evil will happen in my country at my watch." If we don't come together and pray as Christians and come together for the body of Christ we will be divided and no unit and so no faith. Said Zadai. Tell the people you serve a good God. The people of the world will come out and say, we're not having it this way, not on my watch and pray day and night. They will pray and call the angels to come down and support to push out the evil. I cut the root of evil in my country, I cut it off all the evil that are controlling my nation. This is going to happen in the next couple of months and the power of God will take charge and deliver those nations. If people do not pray there will be lawlessness beyond what is happening now and Satan will get to control, the leaders that do not want peace for the people and there will be war between righteousness and evil. God wants us to judge ourselves that we may not be judged by the world. When all things fall apart, it will have nothing to do with our relationship with God rather it's the unfairness of the world. We cannot take it personally it has nothing to do with GOD, so we are being just to accept rejection right now and seek God. We will have God's favor and get ready with oil in our lamp.

God said, "If my people humble themselves and pray, I God will heal their land."

God's plan is to lead righteousness reign and let the justice reign and also have the freedom to speak from the other realm about the Kingdom of God and preach the Kingdom. There are angels all around us and they are ready to go and guide us.

Kevid Zadai said in an interview, "there are three angels right here," standing beside him and Sid Roth. That is the spiritual realm that he sees through. Sid Roth has been talking about God for the last fifty years and Kathryn Kuhlman was once here preaching about the world of God and still he is still preaching the gospel of

Jesus Christ. All these is happening but this is not the end. When the end comes, we will all know it will go to the lawlessness all at once. The generation that Satan is after is in the womb and is the generation that will see the coming of the Lord, they are the voice of the one crying in the desert and they will preach the word of God.

Part Two

Topic Four

Prayer and Praise

LORD, GOD ALMIGHTY, South Sudan exists because of you. What are we, but a puff of smoke? What have the people of South Sudan to you that you have given us independence and land? LORD, God Almighty your love and your plans keep us alive.

LORD, your care and love has brought us out of the civil war. Your love has delivered us from our enemies and given us a country. LORD, God Almighty you have rescued us from the starvation and diseases we faced as a homeless people. You kept us safe from the ambushes of our enemies in the wilderness. You comforted the orphans and widows. You provided food and shelter when there was little hope. You gave us hope, knowing that You are above, watching us. You kept us alive to testify to the world the tales of your miracles in our lives. Your love and power has always been a shining star to the people of South Sudan, and we know that You will always bring a solution to your people. We believe that you love the weak, the disabled, the marginalized, and those who cry daily for your power above to save them. Only You, LORD, stands with the poor, the orphans and the widows. You have taken care of our parents, our ancestors and all living creatures of South Sudan, and now your love and power is still with us. Let us serve you with humility, humbleness in our hearts, love, faith and hope.

We can do nothing without You, LORD. You are the only power we turn to as South Sudanese. We seek your glory, love and power to save your suffering people. We ask you to give our aged strength and hope. We ask you to heal the sick in their homes and in the hospitals, that they be free of their sins and witness your great power. We ask You to forgive our sins and have mercy on the people of South Sudan. We ask You to give us a leader who will serve You and your people, so that peace and prosperity will come to this land You gave us.

LORD, God Almighty may your love continue to unite your people and may we repent of our sins and worship you. May your people build places of worship and may your Glory be seen and witnessed by the whole world and its creatures. May your love and power bless those who call upon your name, and help those who want to know your Word. May all the people of South Sudan worship you and be a testimony of your love and power. LORD, God Almighty, may you continue to bless and protect your children of Israel and those who support their ideas and protect them. Bless your servants and may your love and power be upon them to lead your chosen people well.

LORD God Almighty, we bow down before your kingdom as a country and ask for your glory, love and power to save us from our sins. May your kind heart and mercy be with our children and the children of our children. May they know about you, LORD, and forever serve you in your temple. May your kindness and mercy that has been with us, be with us and our children forever.

The Christian Coalition

Considering the background of war and religion in South Sudan, all Christians should form a coalition to channel their interest and policies in the national government. This can only be achieved if all religions come together for one agenda so as to have a table on the democratic conversation. The lack of Christians rights is what took our fathers to fight for justice and equality of our people. Our grandmothers and fathers in the village grew up knowing little or nothing about Christ Jesus before another generation disappeared. We need to educated our people on religion and as Christians the God in heaven will bless our efforts and He will bless our country, and bless our abandoned resources, hence receiving wisdom and peace to rule with just the population.

We are not creating a state where we have religions competing on the national agenda, but we are creating a religion where freedom and national agenda is passed through churches, mosque, Hindus and crusades. Where those who rule are men and women of integrity of the high caliber. We do not want our religion to be suppressed and we do not want to create a state where Christians suppress other denominations. We will accept freedom of religion and a choice to decide your destiny. Though that does not mean influencing our uneducated youths, women and old aged to serve some individual purpose or other religious purposes other than God.

We follow the gospel of Christ Jesus, the son Of God and the Messiah who is to come. **When the State of Israel recognized our**

independence, they were the first. They did it with good will and with knowledge that becoming a state at this technological world was a challenge.

Israel faced a lot at birth, they did not have a standing army, and operational government. They were only brought together by the United Nations from exile and given their promised land, the land of Abraham, the home of Isaac and the nation of Jacob, though that was their ancestral home. The challenges they faced were numerous and when South Sudan got independent, they understood us as Christians and offered us great support in their national parliament. The Prime Minister allowed us to open our embassy in Jerusalem the capital of Israel.

Sudan was our original home, but due to the fact that our ancestors were not educated and accept to be push further south, we left our ancestral burial site in Khartoum, which natives called, "Khar Tuom" meaning meeting of two rivers. The Arabs slavery and forced Islamic made our ancestors to abandon their land and moved further south with hope they won't be followed. But they were followed, killed and pushed further. When they refuse to move, that brought the civil war that took us fifty years to realize freedom again and to have a state that we rule.

We have lost great fathers and great mothers to the conflicts. The politicians have not been in a position to acknowledge the fallen heroes and heroines of our beloved country, since independence. With the integrity of the churches and their members, we want the rights of such widows, orphans and the poor to be channeled and their rights to be fought by the Christians. The society morals of a child and to keep the mothers secure is and will always be supported by the religion. Through the religious coalition, the politics of abortion will always be put right and the gay politics. I do not deny the existence of such people in the society, they deserve their rights in the society, with respect of liberty, the church and all religions will have a voice to decide the future of such discussions and the fate of it.

The "baby killer" or the sodomites should not be allowed to be religious leaders. The agenda will always be carried by the Christians and strived to unite all Christians to have one agenda for the national interest and one denomination. As Christians, we worship one God and we all follow Christ Jesus as the son of God. That is our base for Christianity so with that, we shall all unite our faith, just as there are many parts in the body and they make up one human being. One body with so many parts functioning for one purpose, so all churches functioning for one purpose. Jesus Christ our Lord. All Christians have one purpose; To serve Jesus Christ and so, to embrace different denominations and operate according to different gifts will be satisfactory for the people of South Sudan and Christ that we both serve.

The name of the church is not the gate way to heaven rather it is the heart that believes and have faith. Faith without action is dead. So, we will wish to safeguard our people and save them but not by making choices for them in faith activities, rather, follow their hearts. They have been strong for a very long time to resist the forced Islamic for five decades of civil war. The tactics might have changed and people might get lost if we do not work as a coalition and with our state government. The religious coalitions should preferably come together and with the guidance of Christ and the Holy Spirit choose a name that will unite them and operate their churches a branched to each other. They will be sharing the readings of each Sabbath day.

South Sudan roots are biblical and with that identity, we need to always thank God for the love and power that He has granted us as a nation and serve him with all our hearts, mind and soul.

Christian manifesto will always guide the national agenda. The Christian coalition will help the restoration of biblical morality in the country. To have salvation is not to believe in God alone but to have faith in Jesus Christ and surrender our souls, heart and mind to him.

Since Christians do not have a table on the conversation of democracy in South Sudan, such coalition will shade light to Christians not to be fooled and hijacked of their rights again as it happened before in Khartoum regime. Going to church does not qualify one as a Christian if one does not follow the Christians norms. Those who do not go to church and follow the norms are better Christians then those who go to church and do not do Christians activities.

As a multi-denominational state, our school-going children need to be taught their religious norms and learn about religion in schools. Every morning parade or classes will always start with a prayer and before they go home after classes, they should end their day with a prayer. As education is the backbone of the economy, religion will be the backbone of our society. The born-again religion should champion the religious rights and build a multi-denominational state but allow the freedom of choice of religion. In the rChristians coalition manifesto, they should make rules that are favorable to other religions and denominations like, Zionism, Hindus, Muslims and others.

Our history should not be wiped out by the independent state, rather we should be more strong. We should show the world why we needed freedom now that we are free people. The agendas that kept our hope and the faith that we had for the last fifty years need to be realized now for the world to see. We had a reason when we fought. That reason is now needed by the world that stood with us to gain independence. The multi-denominational state that fought for independence for five decades is being waited for with the agenda of his people. And this can be passed by the Christians manifesto to the national agenda.

Since we stood just as Israel stood with their culture, language and beliefs, we need to congratulate ourselves as South Sudanese for never accepting to lose our identity, beliefs, language and our traditional norms. That made us strong and united us to face the challenges that lied ahead of us.

The Promised Land

The land divided by rivers, the land of tall, dark and smooth-skin people. The land of the tallest people, found in Africa, mid of East and North Africa and to the East of African continent; the land of South Sudan. the people who since creation of the world have never seen tarmac road. People who have been marginalized and kept their tradition without interaction with the outside world since Ottoman who ruled Northern Africa.

They survived the Ottoman, Anglo-Egyptian, the Nile Civilization, France colonial, the British colonization and the Khartoum regime slavery and marginalization. This land has witnessed all kinds of killing to change them but kept their culture, language and traditional norms and beliefs.

South Sudan is a product of all the wars that have been inflicted on her. They have suffered seeking freedom and safeguarding their traditions. South Sudan is a creation of God and will exist because God wants it to exist for a purpose. The people of South Sudan are chosen people who should all testify the glory of God who saved them from Khartoum regime and gave them a country.

The struggle that has been in phases has witnessed thousands killed. In 1955, the elites of South Sudan took up arms to liberate the Christians South from the Maram regime of Khartoum that saw a peace signed in 1972. That peace brought free movement of Southern Christians till 1983, when Christians were being lynched in various fronts.

1983 saw many South Sudanese taking up arms including pastors in churches. There were defections of soldiers in barracks and public servants. That Christian struggle made southernism to come together regardless of tribes and united as one people to seek their rights. The promised land was demarcated by the colonial powers, who preferred to give powers of the South to the Maram Northerners.

As Israel was led by Moses who saw the promised land and never stepped there, South Sudan was led by Dr. John Garang who saw the land but never set his foot there. The people of Israel were brought to the promised land by Joshua whom God gave authority to lead people to Canaan. The President, just as God gave him the authority, led people of South Sudan to referendum and to the independent state of South Sudan.

Moses died in the mountains after he had seen the promised land, just as Dr. John Garang died in the mountain after he had signed the peace and saw the promised land of the people of South Sudan. God has saved the people of South Sudan and turned the world to support the course and the will of the South Sudanese. When the President took over power, he had anonymous support from the citizens and other countries, Israel, America, Kenya, Norway, Zimbabwe, UK, South Africa, regional and international. South Sudan was the "New Hub of Business" with abandoned resources. The regional traders and international traders were flocking into the country to take up opportunities. South Sudanese government had a good start before they opened their national agenda to the public.

The region and international communities channeled funds to

support the none existent institutions, the country was starting from scratch. There was no infrastructure, no schools building and above all, there were no offices. The government was to start with tents as offices and homes. The funds that were brought were used by military generals to support their broken families and relatives. The first two years saw the country flying out for medication, and educate their children and builds relations with the neighboring countries and abroad.

When they started the national agenda, and opened the national work, they started by looking for witchcraft and witchdoctors. The country's leadership first turned the national agenda and the vision of independence into witchcraft; witchdoctors were consulted about the national affairs and national appointments. They abandoned the LORD, God Almighty who gave them independence and freedom and turned to witches. The money was used to go seek powerful witchdoctors in Darfur, famously known locally as Damazin.

Elders and magicians were transported from the village by looters to come use their magic to get appointment in the government. Witches made no money, but the appointee looted. Those whom their magic worked got enough cattle as payment while others received money. The government abandoned the church and worshipped household gods. The common people never got services and insecurity was worsening on roads and in the city. The land that God gave us, the promised land was turned to be a land where witchcraft dwelled and people worshipped other gods and not Christ Jesus the son of God and the Messiah.

When people went to church, they went to date, and priests talked politics with hatred of other tribes and how government is control by one ethnic community. Politicians went to show their presence and after church called their witchdoctors to strengthen their power to work permanently in the government. Such brought curses and made God angry with the promised land of South Sudanese, hence, the people became angry with each other and killed one another.

God knows that we are not repenting our sins rather we are doing more sins to make the LORD angry. Peace was removed in our land and hatred was planted in our hearts. Communities rose against other communities and butchered one another. Government institutions were used perfect to lift up one society's interest. Whoever got power at the national level used it against the people whom he should protect. The national government became a community government where community matters were addressed by the one who is appointed. People forgot God and the witches bewitched rules.

The country forgot about God and the national agenda was carried by the bewitched who never went to school or were not in the struggle. South Sudan became a breeding ground for the witches and churches were made ceremonially for weddings and Christian holidays. The rest of the days were used to serve other gods.

As the people abandoned God, evil planted hatred and spirit to kill one another, love was nowhere, love that had been there during independence. The people whom no one ever thought could fight each other were on war. They killed each other and burnt churches and homes.

Just as the people of Sodom and Gomorah rejected God and turned to the worldly activities and sinned against God. Divine judgement was passed upon these cities and they were consumed by fire and brimstone. They practiced homosexuality and God was angry with them and when they failed to repent they were punished. South Sudan failed to repent to the Almighty God and the result was civil war. The leadership failed to lead its people to Mt. Zion and accept to repent their sins. The country had the highest immorality, corruption and everyone who went to church came to look for a spiritual traditional leader seeking magical power to get appointment in the government.

There was no reason for the civil war in political differences, but each would consult their witchdoctor if he could win the war and become the country's president. As the witchdoctor was well paid, he would never reject the payer's wishes and that made people go to war with hope to win and let their community have a national pie. The magic has contributed more on the national crisis and people abandoning the true God and church. The people wanted instant results, they never want to go to school to get education, they buy certificates in Uganda and come back seeking witches to authenticate their papers and argue more in the public to prove that they are learned. Their uncles who authenticate their military background with witchdoctors support them and they hold the high posts but they reject God.

This abandoning of God and the church has contributed to the failed peace and stability of the country. Churches have been left empty and people have gone to seek what can help them instantly. The magicians are heard more than common citizen who needs food, security and shelter. The country is literally run by witchcrafts.

In offices and their cars, one can find spears and other magical tools that are believed to bring luck and protect the wealth and power. The more they believe on other gods the more the Almighty God distances Himself from South Sudan and the more the war continues to reign the country. They worship idols and as the Bible say, "You will never serve two masters at ago, you will like one and hate the other." So, the people of South Sudan want to serve two masters; their household gods and the LORD, God Almighty. That will not save South Sudan and will not bring peace to the land. South Sudanese were better off when they were not exposed. Now that they are exposed, they have dropped their culture and got stack between the modern, Arabs culture and their tradition. This can be done if the people of South Sudan turn to the living God and repent their sins. There is no country in the world that can run without strong believers and determination to unite people.

To save our promised land and have prosperity, as believers, we need to turn to God and worship one living God. All churches should come together and destroy all the idols and households' gods in all villages of South Sudan. The leaders that we choose should be God-fearing and have love, faith and hope for a better South Sudan. The qualities of the leaders we should go for should be those true believers with morals and integrity. God bless the people of Israel because they turned to God and repented their sins. God in return blessed their land and the generation of Israel. God of Abraham, Isaac and Jacob is the true God that the people of South Sudan should worship. If we worship Christ Jesus as the son of God and the Messiah we will prosper as a country and peace that we have been longing for the last five years since independence caused by the political unrest will come.

God Almighty does good things to those who worship Him and follow Christian way of life. The righteousness of God is seen on how he creates our beautiful landscape and protects fairly all creatures, none goes without food, not even a lion that feeds on antelope or the antelope that feeds on grass which comes seasonally. God put a man in charge of all the land and all the creatures of the world.

God gives power to the people and if its misused it's taken away and given to another person who will unite and serve the children of God fairly. Dau Alek as a spiritual man has powers invested on him by God and as Jesus said, if someone is doing good in my name he is not against my Kingdom. The same applies to Aguer Dut Athiang who used the power given to him to help the community in all their challenges such as calling rain and saving lives. We can't justify much but as long as they do not kill and do not deny anyone justice, then that is power from God. The same applies to the powers and stories we heard about Ariath Makuei and Athiang Dut Athiang who served God faithfully and help communities.

We have come to the promised land but our idol worship and household gods has denied us to see the fruits of the land God has given us. We have abandoned the church and the living God. It is time for the South Sudanese to abandon those gods and come back to the Creator, the true God that made the universe and located us in this land of Cush. God wants us to anonymously come together and repent our sins at Mt. Zion and build a church down the mountain that we will all worship our God, the God of South Sudanese. God wants us to turn to Him and He will make us eat the fruits of the land he gave us. He will bless the work of our hands and bring adequate rain and bless each household with food and live without fear in the land.

As we all know as Christians, priests are people who are chosen by God and they have certain gifts to teach the word of the LORD, God Almighty. The same applies to the leaders, God will bring us a leader that will unite us and have the wisdom to rule us with justice and integrity. South Sudan has a chance to get peace and be stable if we trust in God. Only God can restore peace, prosperity and bring us a leader that will not cause war but unite us in peace. We have no tribes in front of God we are all his children and a true leader does not see tribes of the citizens of the country rather He sees one people working for the survival of the country's generation.

If we come together as people of South Sudan and worship God, we will build a temple where our God will dwell and He will be our God and we will be His children. Juba will be a historical town and will be left to the tourists and those left to maintain the city and we will all move to the "City of God." In that city, we will always observe Sabbath days and God will be with us and all our prayers will be answered. Whatever one asks and has faith and believes, he will get as our God will be close to listen to us. There will be more Angels then the population in the city.

We are close to the promised land. God will bless us and bring us a leader to lead the country and that will be the entrance of the people of South Sudan to the promised land. The leader will lead us to the temple of God and we will repent our sins and the sins of our ancestors. God will forgive the people of South Sudan and we will be united under the leadership of God's chosen leader. The leader that will unite the people of South Sudan will lead the people in building the "Temple of Peace," the house of God will be the symbol of unity of the people of South Sudan.

Part Three

Topic Five

Christ's Church

THE FOUNDATION OF SOUTH SUDAN is Christianity and religion played a great role in the independence of South Sudan. That made South Sudan a multi-denominational state, secular state in East Africa region. With this knowledge, South Sudan needs to worship the Almighty God wherever they are as a sign of thanksgiving to the LORD for giving us a country. The unity of South Sudanese should be based on faith on the religion. As God takes us as His children and not based on our tribes, we should look at one another as one in Christ and have love for one another.

As we serve our people in different level, we need to pray to God to give us a leader that will unite us and lead us to serve Almighty God better. If we trust in God and pray as one people, we will always have blessings to find one that will lead us into unifying the church and our faith in Christ.

Since there is only one God and our faith is one in Christ Jesus, we should have one church but with many gifted teachers of the words of God. This can make our faith as one and all the churches will be one but many branches. As there is a tree with many branches and the same roots supply nutrition and water to various branches. So is our faith and churches, I suggest, predict, we should have one common name of the church of South Sudan with many branches serving across the country. Catholic church. There is freedom of worship and my suggestion should not limit or control anyone from a diverse freedom of worship and choice of faith. That will make the same word of God to be taught across the churches and that will make our faith strong in Christ Jesus.

We need the people of South Sudan to build one big church that will be a "Peace Temple" a worship center for all faiths. That the people will always ask God for peace and all their needs. The church will be built at the northern part of "Mt. Zion" which the locals currently call "Jebel Lado." The church of Peace of our LORD Jesus Christ will be a unifying temple of God. Here God will always bless us and we will worship God and we will repent our sins and sins of our ancestors at this temple.

As our God dwells at the top of the mountain, we will be serving Almighty God down the mountain at the temple. As the bible said, God dwell at the sacred hill in Jerusalem, the City of God and in Mt. Zion found in Jerusalem. We should serve God at this temple in South Sudan as we keep the Christians beliefs and norms. We should target a temple that holds ten thousand people with residential of the people who serve God our LORD. This temple will bring peace to the people of South Sudan and the world.

We need to build a worshipping place at the top of the mountain.

An open place where public can go up using a lift machine. At the top, will be a well cemented space for the public and a reception and a gate. The reception will be a small gate, walk through. And the main gate, just like a car gate. The priest and the leaders of the people will be going through the reception to ask God about the people they lead. The main gate will be open thrice a year to the public and could be open in time of pandemic that has hit the country or the world.

The reception will be like the gate to heaven and the same will applies with the main gate. The public space will be open throughout the year for the public to always worship God anytime of their wish. The tax got at the lift that takes people up the mountain or those who walk up, will be used for supporting the temple, orphans, old age and widows.

The Trinity

The trinity holds that God is one God, hence lives in three coeternal consubstantial persons, The Father, the Son and the Holy Spirit. That is one God in three Divine persons.

A good Christian should have the three virtues to be accepted in the Kingdom of God, Love, Faith and Hope. Knowing that faith without action is dead. The greatest of the three virtues is Love. The Hope come first, faith is based on hope, to hope in the future life and then have faith that it will be done as you hope.

1. Love
2. Hope
3. Faith

Love

Love is the greatest weapon in the world that breaks borders between ordinary and great leaders. Love is the secret code that bring together people of all races, tribes and nations for a common course. Love unites people and breaks hatred, love is patient and cares, love is persistent and carries a vision and a mission for peace. Love made God to give His son Jesus Christ to save the world. Love made Jesus to sacrifice his soul and died on the cross for our sins. He did it for the sake of the human race to be saved and follow the love of God.

With love, all things are possible, love brings the country together as one and provides service to the citizens equally. A country that is united by love does not have her citizens in refugee camps and in exile. Love unites and brings peace. Love is what makes a mother to cry about her child when the child is sick, she loves and cry, she prays for the safety of her child, for the love she has for her child. The mother love is strong, straight from heaven, she understands only her can love her child and provide for her. God love is above all loves in the world.

Famine and Love

During the famine of 1988 in South Sudan, the South Sudanese were rebelling against the government in Khartoum and so, there was little food supply to the people of South Sudan. There was a family located at the edge of the village of Warawar a commercial Centre for the residents of Aweil East. The head of the family was named Akot Akuel. He had a wife named, Along. They just got married and the wife was pregnant with their first child. They lived happily. The family was a cattle keeper and had a shop at the commercial center of Warawar.

Akot live with his wife and his mother Aluat in a two huts compound. They were at the edge of the village so they farmed towards the forest where many gwent to collect firewood. One summer, the Arab attackers came and raided the village taking with them cattle and burning down all the granaries of sorghums. The next season was five mothers away. The village had just harvested and they lost all their daily incomes to the conflicts.

The youth of the village came together and formed "Gel Weng" to protect the village from such attacks. The Sudan People's Liberation Army was not yet formed. The 'Gel Weng' movement was the new organized armed rebellion that was spreading to the countryside. Akot and his colleagues came together and they formed a unite of Gel Weng to defend their village from the raiders.

The youths came together and a built base in Ang'oot, another town north of Warawar, towards the border where the attackers came from. Ang'oot was fifty kilometers away from Warawar and so, families were left with women to take care of the households.

Along was left with her mother-in-law and she was left with three months to delivery. Rainy seasons were five months away. Single handedly, she had to find ways to fend for the family's survival. The mother-in-law was blind and could not move around or work. That year saw many families abandon their homes and left for Khartoum. Though the news coming from there said, those who went to Khartoum became Muslims. One scary story to a typical Dinka. What scared them most is the conspiracy of tattoo mark at the buttock, and above all the slavery. But there are those who preferred slavery and tattoo mark to dying of hunger.

Along was forced to open a coffee shop where she sold coffee and fried groundnuts. If the market was bad and she did not sell anything, then they would eat the goods that were supposed to be for the market. Months elapses and Along gave birth to a bouncing baby boy, she named him Garang, which means the first man to have been created by God (Adam). After two weeks, they had eaten all the groundnuts and they closed the shop. They were left to starved to death as there was nothing left to eat.

Along had just given birth and there was no one to attend to her. The mother-in-law was stuck in the house as she needed guidance to move. In the house, there was only a quarter kilogram of salt left and empty cooking pots. The mother-in-law had been asking for food for the last three days and nothing was forthcoming. The pain Along had could not even allow her to go to the forest to get some tree leaves and come and cook. She is growing weak as days goes.

Every homestead was empty either they left for Khartoum or they joined the Gel Weng where they looted villages for their survival and kept watch of the enemy. Along and the blind mother-in-law had nowhere to go but wait for death to knock at their door. They were growing weak each day. On the fourth day, they thought to kill the baby and eat him. The mother-in-law suggested and Along was not satisfied with the suggestion. So, the mother-in-law said, then my daughter, kill me and have something to eat with your baby, after all, I am aged now, there is no need for me to live.

Along was not okay with that either. What would she tell her husband if he comes back? That she ate the mother-in-law that will be an abomination. She rejected it and said, 'mother, we will both die together so there will be no witness of one killing the other one. Hope has vanished, love was hanging on a string and faith had deserted their household days ago. They were living dead.

On the fifth day, as they sat next to the fire, there was no talking and the baby was crying. The mother gave him breast but there was nothing coming out. Breast feeding the baby was making the mother weaker.

Along decided in her heart that she will kill the baby to save herself and the mother-in-law. She would take the baby close to the fire, then drop him and roast him. When the baby feels the heat of the fire, she will laugh at the mother and smile with a tender love. Then the mother would lift him up again. When the mother put her to her laps he will continue to cry. And if she returns her close to the fire, she will smile back to her mother and show some tender love to the mother.

Along tried that thrice, as she tried to burn the baby Garang and have him for lunch and dinner. The door was open when an antelope came running, being chased by a lion, they guessed, because they do not know what sent the antelope into their hut. The antelope jumped into the fire and hit his head at the wall behind and lay there half dead. The antelope was already weak and exhausted. Along placed the baby Garang on the bed and hit the antelope on the neck killing it instantly. By the time the blind mother-in-law asked what it was, the antelope was already dead. She explained as she cut some pieces and roast it to save their lives and the life of the little baby. They ate the first pieces with blood, the meat only test the fire.

The baby had been saved by the antelope, he was probably the easy meal that they could have had for the day without complain. God provided them with a meal and something to eat for mothers till the rains came. They had to ratio the meat for the next remaining two months. They could also get tree leaves to change the diets. The love of the mother could not let the baby die and even if things were hard and their lives were at the gate of death, love for the baby could not let her drop her baby in fire. The love of God was above all the loves; He gave them another meal for God loves his people.

The love and care for the mother-in-law was so strong, Along, thought of what she will tell her husband. She cares more about the husband love's and what people will say if she survived the famine. God's love was above all and the angel of God was with them. God knew what they were going through and He provided for them food to their door step. God cares and He loves, He knows our daily needs and He brings first what we need the most. God's love comes with time and his right time is always to prove to us His strength, love and care for us. God gave us hope and with faith, he provides to us all our needs through prayers.

Hope and Faith

Faith is the acceptance and having confidence of unseen things. We hope on what we have faith on. "Faith can move a mountain" as said in the bible by Christ Jesus. Faith comes before action; with faith, you have the picture of what you want and how you will get it. Faith is the means to our dreams. With faith, all things are half done and it needs action to have it completed. Faith gives the means and determination and a complete image of the end results.

Hope is what you desire and form the image of it and it takes faith and action to have your hope come true. Hope is the feeling of desire and expectation, and that can be completed by faith and action. Hope approach problems with a strategy and with a mindset to achieve it and faith is the believe that you will make it succeed.

A Family Formed Through Faith and Hope

When two people fall in love and get married, the foundation of the family is through faith that they will have healthy children, raise them and continue their family lineage. They believe that they will have a happy family and raise their children in a peaceful and secure family. Teach them norms and beliefs of the society. They hope that all shall be well, if they have faith and take action on their duties.

In the countryside, town of Warawar, South Sudan. There was

a young man called Joseph, he was a son of the paramount chief Achom. Joseph was a Christian, he attended missionary church his father introduced him to and he was baptized and joined the local school before he went to Meram for further studies. He went to Meram to study and when he came back at the age at which he should get married, his father called for a function in their house for him to pick a girl of his choice among the most beautiful girls of the village. All the girls came and Joseph was not satisfied with all that he saw. The function went on; food was distributed to all the visitors. Many came across the region, neighboring communities with their paramount chiefs sent their daughters. When evening came and Joseph had not made up his mind, the event was about to be closed when this young and beautiful girl came. She was late as she had to cook at home, fetch water and get firewood before she went out to the event as she would come home late after event, when no one can go to get firewood.

Her name was Mary, a daughter of the prominent community spiritual leader. She was from the lineage of a prophet Dau Alek. From a distance, Joseph fixed his eyes on her till she was close. The young girl came and stood behind the crowd and watched the dances and plays. Joseph approached her, asked her name and asked her out. That became his choice for marriage. Mary was a daughter of the spear-master of the village. She had been taught all kinds of traditions and care for the family. She knew all norms and beliefs. The preparation for the wedding was done, Joseph was the next heir of his father's chiefdom.

The wedding was prepared and the family of Mary was paid thirty cattle as a bride price. On the wedding day, all the seven paramount chiefs of that region were invited and the wedding was done in a traditional way. Three days of wedding as traditions required. It took three days for the event to get over, including agreement on the bride price, goodwill for the mother-in-law and goodwill for the groom's friends and the step-mothers. After the wedding, Mary was left in her home with an assistance girl, who will help her in house chores.

In a couple of months, she was pregnant and that was the joy of those who attended her wedding. Villagers had been asking when she would be pregnant and have her child. This is always the pride of the mother to see her daughter contributing to the family lineage of that clan she got married to. Mary gave birth and raised her lovely baby boy well and healthy. There was peace in the country and business was booming in the local commercial center of Warawar.

They were living happily in a two-bedroom house in Auchier estate. The husband was a businessman and the wife was taking care of goats and cattle in the homestead. They were the admirable family in the town. Joseph being educated, he raised his child in a modern manner. He was there for his wife and child. He provided for his family and showed love to his beautiful wife.

Two years and half down the line, the young Robert stopped breastfeeding, Mary was pregnant again and she has experienced now, so, she could take care of herself and the little boy, Robert. When she was about to give birth, her husband had already joined the rebellion in the region, they were fighting the government forces that came to attack their commercial center and loot properties.

When Mary gave birth for her second child, Joseph was not there. He was in the wilderness hiding from the government troops that came to kill the youths and those that were able in the village, else change them into Islamic. Joseph was setting ambushes and attacks on government troops. Mary was assisted by her mother-in-law to deliver her second bouncing baby boy, David. On the day of her delivery, there was an attack in the village that she had to run into the forest with a new born baby boy. She spent days in a chilling cold weather of autumn. Survival was paramount then they had to endure the chilly weather.

When she came back home, there was no granaries, the barns of grains were burnt, cattle were gone, goats and sheep were no more. The wall of the house was left in the compound with ashes on them after fire blazed the roofs down. Mary had to start again by looking for food and cutting grass to thatch her house for the rains were near, the winter season. Moreover, Mary was to prepare food and take to the military barrack where her husband was hiding in the forest, fifty kilometers away from home. She had to take lunch daily after a hard hustle of looking for grains to grind and cook.

After two months of the same routines, Joseph left for Ethiopia giving a break to the hard walk and hustle for food by Mary for him and his men. Mary had to take care of her two children and the mother-in-law who was staying with her. The family was broken apart by the civil war. The mother with the children and no husband. Her father-in-law was killed by the Arabs and that is what made her husband to abandon the family and join the war for freedom. There was no love at sight and the struggle for survival dominated their minds in a civil war environment. Mary turned to the local brews, she prepared them as there was high demand for consumption. Aregi, asilia and mou heer were the common brews asked by many in the village. She prepared the brews and sold them to raise her children.

Aregi, asilia and mou heer were all ordered simultaneously by the constantly impatient customers. Her home was where all the rebellion was planned, attack and overthrowing the government after they were tipsy. The drunkards knew how to plan when tipsy and formed a united government. Many who rebelled were driven by aregi or mou heer and when the "mou" (beer) is over on their heads, they found themselves in the barrack and no retreat as they could go and spy against the rebellion. While those who were annoyed with the poor leadership carried the agenda of rebellion.

During the famous famine of 1988, she was still selling her local brews in Warawar market. The years after, there was intensity of attacks and blazing of homes and the market. That was to chase away the villagers from their ancestral homes. Many on that year left for Khartoum and Mary decided to follow her husband to Ethiopia. Many young men left to Ethiopia seeking military training and came back to fight the Arab attackers. Mary joined them with her two sons, her two brothers and her sister. In a group of a hundred and twenty people, there was only one AK-47 that was protecting them all. There were no guns and so, the one gun was always placed in front to defend and secure the way as they moved.

None of them knew the way to Ethiopia, they asked for direction from any village they came across. Before they got to Ethiopia, they came across a military barrack and luckily, it was for the South Sudanese and so there were no fights. They spent a night and next day before they left, the commander of the barrack forcefully married Mary's sister, Magdalene. He took her and said, she will remain there as his wife, Mary was forced to abandon her sister and continue with her journey to Ethiopia.

When Mary got to Ethiopia, she found her husband in prison accused by the rebel leaders for being indiscipline in the military barrack. She spent days in the refugee camps while arrangements were being made for her to go and see her husband in the prison with her two grown boys. Weeks later, she was taken to an island prison by Garang Ateny, where her husband had been for the last eight months. They spent one week in a house prison in the island then Mary returned to the refugee camp and stayed there for two years with her children.

Again, the political situation of the host country and the rebel group of South Sudan was unstable and the refugees were to move back to South Sudan. Mary with her sons were to walk for another six months to Bahr el Ghazal region. This time it would take them a year as they dodged towns that were occupied by the government forces. The attacks were countless but this time it was better as the husband, Joseph was there. They came towards Kenya, Uganda border and then moved upwards towards Central Africa Republic and then to the northern Bahr el Ghazal region.

Joseph was made the commander of Bahr el Ghazal barrack, based in Awiel after his release from prison. The broken family was back together once again. What kept them together was faith, hope and determination. They lived happily thereafter in the region of Awiel and raised their young boys. Robert and David joined a school and finished their education till university after peace was signed in 2005. David was into politics and wanted to make a difference in the lives of those who had suffering in the civil war, the mothers and disabled people in the society.

Robert joined the aviation industry as he was so interested and he became a pilot. Now it was the faith and hope that the mother had to raise them that made the difference in their lives. Now the faith and hope is on them to support their old mother and father. The peace was earned by their father who had been shot several times and survived them all. The hope is on the young children to serve the country and the people of South Sudan. Faith and hope have helped them survive the hardship and now the family hopes that the boys will continue the family lineage and raise their families well and serve God as their father and mother did.

My God, God of my Father, Mother and Grandparents

God of my ancestors, Abraham, Isaac and Jacob, God of my father, God of my mother, God of my grandfather and God of my grandmother help us. We worship Christ as Messiah and the son of God, the living God of Israeli and South Sudanese. I pray to my God to have mercy on his people and give them peace, a leader like your servant King David and a wise leader like King Solomon and a faithful friend like your friend Abraham, LORD.

God, LORD you are my God my savoir. You have been good to me since I was born. LORD, you protected me in my life time since I was young. LORD, I have never met any danger at night or during the day. You watch over me, my foot steps and decisions that I make, that is the glory of God that has been walking with me, my LORD, God of my father, God of my mother and God of my ancestors.

Your constant love LORD has protected me in the civil war where I lost many of my generation. I have heard war, I have heard deaths, but LORD you have prevented and protected me from witnessing them in my life. Your constant love LORD has saved me from trauma and horror of the massacre in my country. Your constant love has made me forgive my enemies and we reconcile as members of Christ's Kingdom. Your glory God has always been with me and within my surrounding, I feel your presence.

LORD, I have never lacked food and shelter, your powers and the glory above have always provided me my desires. LORD, you control my thoughts and wishes so as the will of God may be done in me and through me. You give me what my heart desires, one that will benefit others, thank you LORD, my God. I will always be a testimony of your glory to the Christian community and all the believers of the world.

LORD, you have saved me from my enemies, you have always made me win over those who plan evil against me. LORD, because of your constant love and care, all dangerous things happen before I reach the danger or they will happen after I have left the site. Your constant love and care LORD have never made me meet any danger in my life. You have always saved me from all horrors and disasters of the world we live. Your glory has always guided me, your angels have never left my side and they protect me, provide for me and lead me on the right path, LORD.

Your Holy Spirit, LORD has never abandoned me, just as you promise us Holy Spirit, LORD, you send them and now they are the guiding light on our daily path. They provide us with our daily needs and they lead us on the right path as we seek you LORD, God the Father. Your angels have given me wisdom, understanding and knowledge as you said LORD, ask and you will be given, knock and the door will be open to you, seek and you will get. LORD, your glory is always constant with me everywhere I go. I thank you LORD, my Father God that your son Jesus Christ came to rescue us from our sins. I pray in faith and hope LORD and you have always answered my prayers through the blood of Jesus Christ.

Since I was young LORD, I have always sought your Kingdom, I thirst for the knowledge of the Kingdom of God. You have never let your servant down ever since I was born. I ask and you give me LORD, I knock and the door have always been open to me and when I seek I always found your kingdom ready to receive me LORD, God my Father. You have been listening to your servant prayers LORD and may your Holy Spirit, your angels continue to support me and support my family and friends. May those who read this be blessed and learn the will of God and worship you LORD. I seek your glory LORD and the same is what every Christians seek, the glory of God to guide us, lead us and protect us now and forever.

May you bless my children and guide, protect them Lord God, to love you, follow for the rest of their lives. Provide for my children and may they worship you forever Lord.

LORD, may your plans in my life be reveal and may the angels tasked to guide me daily fulfil the will of God and may the God of God be with us forever. May I do the work of my LORD Jesus for the rest of my life and my children's lives. Thanks for your Guardian angels LORD, through them I have learnt every day and they have protected me and led me on the right path. I worship you Father God, my Father in Heaven. I follow you LORD Jesus, the Messiah and the son of God. LORD, may I worship you to the end of this universe and go to your kingdom. In faith, I will walk to Heaven like your prophet Elijah. In faith and hope all is possible in your Kingdom and those who seek you LORD.

LORD, may your glory be seen at the top of the mountain in South Sudan. May your glory be witnessed by the South Sudanese and the people of the world LORD, at the top of the mountain and may they bow down to worship you LORD, God my Father in Heaven. May I bring your people of South Sudan together to repent their sins and worship you at Mt. Zion, your sacred Hill LORD, where you dwelled even before we were born. Where our ancestors worship you LORD, at a City of your Servant King David. May we worship you in the Temple LORD, God Almighty.

Thank you, LORD that you have been so kind to me, your constant love has been so great, your wisdom and knowledge has guided me through my enemies and led me on the right path away from danger. I seek justice and peace for the people of South Sudan. Mothers and children are crying day and night seeking your glory and freedom from your temple LORD. LORD, elders, the aged both women, children and men are looking for rest LORD and only you can give that rest through your constant love and your glory LORD. They have suffered and they have never got peace in their lives, only the dead find rest, but the dead LORD, will never thank you in their graves. May you save our mothers, fathers and innocent children from all danger and may they find peace in your temple and on the land, you gave us LORD, so we can praise your name and worship you my friend, my Lord Jesus.

May your constant love be with us forever LORD, may we worship you forever, God of South Sudan, the Living God of Abraham, God of Isaac and God of Jacob. May we continue to worship you as our ancestors obey your laws and worship you LORD, God of Israel. May the whole world with all its creatures bow down and worship. May all South Sudanese bow down and worship you God, the creator of the universe and all its inhabitants. Thank you LORD for wisdom, understanding and knowledge and may I unite the people of South Sudan and bring them into your Temple to worship you LORD, my God and my Father in Heaven.

LORD, may you keep my parents safe, so that I may reveal the glory of God to them. LORD, may I teach the people of South Sudan the glory and the message of our LORD Jesus Christ and may they see the glory of God at the top of the mountain before they leave this earth. May all the aged of South Sudan stay alive LORD, that the word of God be shown to them and worship you LORD, my God. LORD, may the people of South Sudan testify to the world that you alone LORD is God and that you alone saved them from their enemies and gave them a country. May they confess LORD that there is only one God and there is no other God with glory like our God. I devote my life to serve you LORD and to worship you forever. May your angels guide me and lead me on the right path to glory of God.

God please help the innocent people in South Sudan and across the world, deliver them from their struggles, may they see your glory and turn to you LORD. May peace come to the people of South Sudan and the region, bring peace to all the regions and the world around. May your people of Israel continue to serve you and LORD give them peace, they are your chosen nation. I pray LORD that you may help, protect and provide to all the mothers in the world and the orphans and all the children who need your support LORD. You alone Father can help and save lives. May peace continue to prevail in South Sudan and may the people find a leader that will unite them and protect and deliver people to your temple LORD to worship you.

The Deliverance of the People

The people of South Sudan are lost and need to be found, all Christians who do not follow the will of God are lost and they can only be delivered by the blood of Jesus Christ. When we talk of the deliverance of the people of South Sudan. That is the act of setting people of South Sudan free from spiritual bondages and barriers that hold them back in seeing light and enjoying the victory of Jesus Christ on the cross and be part of the victory.

South Sudanese have been suppressed and denied the chance to see the light and learn the word of God for so many years. That means, they have been under Satan's power worshiping their idols and sacrificing bulls to their gods for ages. Now the Christians community in the world need to come together and support the few pastors and priests to preach the word of our Lordship Jesus Christ.

The people we are trying to deliver to our LORD Jesus Christ are people who have no knowledge about our Lord Jesus' sacrifice on the cross. As the bible says, those who have no knowledge of our God needs to be fed with milk and not solid food. The people of South Sudan need to be given milk to know the truth and to know

Christ Jesus. A mother in the village, countryside has never heard the name Jesus Christ. And if they might have heard of it, then they do not know why he had to die on the cross and who killed him.

The word of our LORD Jesus should not be taught like colonial history that has no benefits in our lives or be taught like any past history of our ancestors. Jesus Christ is a savior, and the son of God, who died that for our sins and prepare our path to heaven. Church has been made like a ceremonial place that people go not to learn but to meet friends and after church, people turn to their traditional beliefs and norms. Our spiritual leaders in church need to guide our people and engage them to let the word of God sink in their hearts and create desire in them to learn and follow the word of God.

Deliverance of our people is a great task that everyone should play a role at each one's capacity that Jesus be in our heart, mind and soul in South Sudan. If we can deliver Lord and invite the Kingdom to our heart and soul, then Christ will dwell in South Sudan and he will deliver peace and all that our people ask for. The kingdom of God is coming soon and we need to save our people and the earlier they know the word of Living God the better for our generation and the generation after. The Mother of God, the Virgin Mary will always pray and give us Mother's love always. Our people are left behind in knowing the word of God, but God has been patient and feeding us with milk until when we are ready to eat solid food. The world has already known about the Lord but our people are still worshipping other gods.

A mother in the countryside lives forty kilometers to and fro, away from the nearby church. They have to trek each Sunday to learn the word of the living. God, her children never miss a church and her daughter is always in the church choirs. Her son is always those outgrow youths who feel that church is for the children, and if she attends a church it will be a Christian holiday such as Easter or Christmas. The mother herself rarely go to church. She is always left home to cook and take care of house chores. Those who go to church cannot come and teach others as they did not go to listen and learn rather, they went to show their present.

This culture can be changed if we change the way we teach our people about Christ. The basic lesson is that we need to change from home gods and accept Christ in our houses and whatever we do at home must be Christianly accepted. We should teach our people to stop sacrificing animals to idols and other gods. That is the beginning of accepting Christ in your life. The bible starts from the basic Christians norms and beliefs. A country that turns to God and worships God is always blessed with peace and prosperity. The distance at which our people have to walk to church is long, but that shows great commitment if only they are taught right, they can learn and change to do the right thing of serving God.

The deliverance of the people of South Sudan is very vital and that should be our role as citizens of South Sudan, those in the leadership and the ordinary, in God we are all equal and his children. Accepting Christ should be our primary role and the beginning of knowing the Kingdom of God. The only way we can change the hardship of knowing Christ in the countryside is by adding more churches for our people to access them. Training more pastors to deliver the word of God so that no one is left lost and that God will help us achieve our wish of bringing the people of South Sudan to his glory. The churches should be having national funding so that the state institutions support in the spread of the word of God to the communities in South Sudan.

We have been awarded with peace by our Lord Jesus Christ, and now the Lord needs us to turn to him and worship him. Those who have gone to school to study theology should lead our Christian population and guide them to know our Lord Jesus. There are those who are born gifted with preaching and there are those who learn as the Bible say, the same spirit gives different gifts to human beings, let's use our gifts for the good of our God to spread his word. I acknowledge that our people are thirsty to know the word of God but its upon us to guide them else, others will mislead them and take them to other gods and not to Christ. If we take an initiative to take our people on the right path, we will be blessed and our country will prosper with the blessing from son of God, Jesus.

Those who seek God are blessed by God and those who reject God are rejected by God. We want to seek God and get the blessing of our Lord and our Father in Heaven.

There is a story in the bible about the Covenant Box of God. **2 Samuel 6:1-23**

When King David wanted to bring the Covenant Box to Jerusalem, he sacrificed a lot of bulls to God initiated by the priest of God. There was singing and dancing as four people carried the Covenant Box. On their way, one of the people who was crying the Covenant Box stumbled down and he died instantly. That brought fear to King David and those who were carrying the Covenant Box. Then King David thought may be God was not happy and so he decided to have the covenant Box at the nearby house of one of the Jews family.

After three months, news came to King David that the Covenant Box had blessed the house at which it was kept. That family now became rich and God blessed them with many cattle, goats and sheep. When King David heard the news, he ordered for the Covenant Box to be brought to Jerusalem. He went with more bulls to be sacrifice to God, he called for the clan of Levi to lead the worship of the LORD and he was there as servant of God and not as king. He danced and sang as the Covenant Box was being brought to Jerusalem. He did this to seek the blessing of God and be blessed with wealth and his kingdom be blessed to lead his people.

Each nation seeks blessing of God for her people to prosper. South Sudan should seek the blessing of God by uniting the people and deliver them to serve God and worship Him for the rest of their lives. There is no nation that can prosper without God.

South Sudan should bring all prophets of the world, pastors and all priests to come and worship in South Sudan. This should be a national initiative by the leadership and spiritual leaders to seek God glory and build a foundation that will unite all Christians. This initiative will be the foundation of deliverance of the people of South Sudan. If all the prophets of the world, priests of the world and the pastors of the world are brought together in South Sudan, we will see changes and God will listen to his children and that will bring peace and prosperity to the land. The promised land that God promised us will be blessed and our children will live in the land secure and with love.

Those who need more teachings are our mothers and young children in the countryside where the word of God has not reached. These are the people who need to see the light of God and His glory. They need more churches and schools; they need more priests and spiritual leaders to teach them in their language slowly to understand the message of our Lord Jesus. The country is suffering from the civil war but the word of God has love and peace. If they have the opportunity to know the word of God, they will use the word to bring peace and they will not have to use the gun to bring order. Our people needs more churches and not more military barracks or cantonment zones. If they are taught the word of God, there will be less killing as the word of God teaches us to love and not to kill.

Learning from Suffering of Our LORD Jesus Christ

Christ Jesus is the Messiah and the son of God. He was crucified on the cross to save the universe from their sins. Jesus died on the cross that people might be forgiven their sins through repentance of sins. He was crucified and died and on the third day he rose back to life. He conquered death and through him all that believe in him will not die but live with him in the Kingdom of God.

Before Jesus was crucified, he performed many miracles. The first miracle of his ministry was in a wedding in Nazareth. There was a wedding and the wine had finished and there were more guests who had not got wine. Jesus' mother came to him and told him, "son the wine is over and there are more guests and no wine." "my time or my hour has not yet come, mother." Jesus said. Then he decided to perform miracles, he asked for all the pots of wine to be filled with water and Jesus said, "take a cup and take it to the master of the ceremony to taste." When the master of the ceremony tested, he said, how did you hide the good wine until the guests are about to get drunk and you remove it late. He was not aware that a miracle had been done. That was the first miracle recorded in the bible as performed by our LORD Jesus.

Jesus healed blind men and raised the death and had a lot of followers. People believed in him as the Messiah and as the son of God. What he did amazed people and having known prophets of God assist. Jesus was more powerful than all the prophets that might have existed before. As many people followed him to listen to his message and heal them from various diseases, he attracted more citizens of Jews, Samaria and Gentiles.

We are told that he fed five thousand men and not counting the women and children. And what we can learn is that, when Jesus was crucified, all the people that followed him were nowhere to stand with him and testify that he was a good man. Even his own disciples abandoned him and tried to save themselves from the ruler of the earth. We can be sure that, only God stands with us and when we do good to people, those can be forgotten but with God, all good deeds are rewarded. The people never remembered to defend Jesus who saved them, healed the sick and raised the dead. God who he did all these good miracles and whom he preached never abandoned him. Almighty God whom he served stood with him on the cross and delivered him from the world of death.

Jesus Christ came as human being and the chosen one of God to wash away our sins and deliver us from the world of dead to the Kingdom of God. When Christ was mocked, and beaten by the Roman soldiers, all the people whom he healed, those whom he rose from the dead and the blind that he opened their eyes watched from a distance. We all should learn that God work rewards but the human work is only to please the flesh. The shame he had to endure for the sake of mankind and because Jesus knew he was doing it for the Father who sent him, He accepted to be publicly ashamed and killed.

The soldiers asked him, "you save so many people, why don't you save yourself from the cross." But Jesus did not want to be a hero by walking out from the cross, Jesus knew that he had to fulfill the work of the Father in Heaven and he had to suffer and rose from the dead as the scripture says. The power was on the cross and Him conquering the world of the dead. Christ was publicly mocked and ashamed but what he was to win was bigger than the miracles the people were asking of him. He had performed miracles and they did not believe in him, he rose the dead to life, healed the deaf and the blind but the target of the LORD was his mission on earth and not to prove himself to the none believers' demands.

We should learn and accept that Jesus Christ died on the cross because of our sins. He was humiliated and he accepted it because of his constant love for us. We need to repent our sins and the sins of our ancestors and worship him, the Lord. The only way we will relieve him from pain is by worshipping God our father who gave his son to suffer that we may be delivered from the world of dead. Amen.

We are Christian with no church; South Sudan need help from all Christians of the world, to build a temple of God. Let's help spread the word of God.

Amen.

www.ingramcontent.com/pod-product-compliance
Lightning Source LLC
Chambersburg PA
CBHW020522120726
47904CB00003B/929